THE FINDER AND THE KEEPER

VANESSA GRAY BARTAL

DRY CREEK PRESS

PROLOGUE

C ameron Ridge knew it was bad news the moment The Colonel stepped into his office.

"How's Maggie?"

"Uncomfortable," Ridge answered, his chest tightening with anxiety. The Colonel never began with personal questions. They were always secondary, after whatever the day's crisis might be.

"Heading to Texas anytime soon?"

Two personal questions. Ridge did a quick mental inventory of how many nuclear codes must have leaked for things to be this dire. "Not until after the baby. Apparently women aren't allowed to fly this close to the end."

"Not commercially, but I could probably pull some strings, get you on a military flight, if Maggie wanted. I know Bailey would love to see her again, Cal, too."

Oh, sweet mercy, the world must be ending. Finally Ridge could take it no longer. "Sir, what's this about?"

The Colonel took a breath, reached inside his jacket, and placed a picture on the table between them. Ridge studied it, not certain what he was looking for. There were two pictures, one atop the other, a street scene with a few subtle differences between them.

"I'm sorry, sir, what am I looking at?" he asked after not being able to figure it out.

"A contest."

Ridge's answering frown became mixed with confused blinks. "A contest, sir? I'm not certain I understand. Terrorist recruitment?"

"Something like that. Some lame brain at the CIA had the clever idea to open a contest to civilians, to see how many could spot the differences in these two pictures."

"You must be joking," Ridge said. Espionage was about so much more than being observant, although that helped.

"Yes, Lieutenant, I'm a laugh riot," The Colonel groused. He pushed the picture closer to Ridge. "How many differences do you spot?"

Ridge picked it up and studied it a minute. "Ten, no, eleven."

"I caught thirteen," The Colonel said.

Ridge blinked at him, waiting for more. He didn't have to wait long.

"The person who won the contest found twenty seven."

Ridge looked at the picture again. No. No way were there twenty seven differences between the two pictures. "That's not possible."

"She looked at it under an electron microscope and counted pixels," The Colonel said. "And that only counted as one of the differences."

"Wow, okay. Good for her, I guess? But by your presence here, I'm somehow guessing it's bad for us."

"You know I haven't made a lot of friends on Capitol Hill."

Ridge nodded his agreement. The Colonel straddled the gap between Congress and the military, trying to bring street sense and a hands-on approach to politicians and bureaucrats who often had zero understanding of what it was actually like to be a soldier or spy. He was a ruthless bulldog when it came to speaking his mind, trying to work in favor of the person who had to do the hands-on work of intelligence gathering. Often this put him at odds with the politicians.

"As a way to take their revenge, they've put this on me, handed me their civilian like some kind of untrained pet."

"I assume she's been to Quantico," Ridge said. Everyone had to go to Quantico, even his librarian wife had spent twenty weeks there.

"You assume wrong," The Colonel bit out.

"Wait a minute, they're giving us a civilian fresh off the street and expecting us to train her on the job? A job that could get her killed?" Ridge said, incredulous. Politicians came up with some doozies sometimes, but this was a reach, even for them.

"Oh, it gets worse." The Colonel took a breath. "They've given her a handler."

"A handler," Ridge repeated. Obviously he knew what a handler was, but his incredulity made him unable to process the word as it related to his current situation.

"Someone to babysit her fulltime and keep her safe, make certain she doesn't stumble into trouble for a while until she gets acclimated," The Colonel said.

"Please tell me they're not pulling someone from my team to babysit," Ridge replied. Their team had finally reached a level of cohesive perfection he hadn't felt since he left the SEALs. It would be like the government to mess it up when things were finally perfect.

"No, they're not pulling someone from your team to babysit. But I will be adding the rookie and her handler to your team. With Maggie leaving soon, she might be an asset here, if we can get her properly trained."

"And the handler?" Ridge said.

The Colonel met his look without blinking. "Is someone you already know."

Ridge sifted his mind for possibilities. By now he knew The Colonel well enough to understand this was bad news, dire even. Who would be such a bad addition to his team it was enough to make The Colonel sound apologetic? And suddenly Ridge knew.

"No, sir, not him."

"Yes, Lieutenant. Him."

CHAPTER 1

L eo Holland woke with the feeling that he had forgotten something. But since he always woke with that feeling, he ignored it and reached for whatever drink was on the table beside his bed. Grimacing, he sat up and tried to work the kinks from his body. Getting old was brutal. Technically thirty two wasn't old, but Leo had lived fast and hard and his body showed all the signs of giving in and giving out. His back ached all the time now, as did his knees. Even his hips had started to hurt.

His glance slid around his shabby room—bare mattress, one sweaty wadded blanket, a broken chair draped with a week's worth of laundry. Beneath that, his phone now buzzed insistently. He considered ignoring the phone, but no one except work would contact him at this hour, or any hour, really. Haphazardly, he tossed the clothes onto the floor and reached for his phone, swiping it with his thumb as he said a mumbled greeting.

"Boy, if you are not in your car and halfway to the airport before I finish speaking this sentence, I will come through the phone and snap what's left of your neck."

The call ended as Leo dove for his pants and skidded to the hall-way, hopping on one foot as he paused to put them on. Only The

Colonel could inspire the sort of fear Leo now felt. He *had* forgotten something, something important. His new assignment, the girl.

Cursing, he sprinted down the stairs and jumped in his car, using the wipers to push away the accumulated parking tickets. They were more of a suggestion, really. Technically he was in law enforcement. Shouldn't that buy him some leeway with parking? He might have an emergency, like now when he forgot where he was supposed to be.

The drive to the airport was its usual nightmare. He skidded to a halt in the no parking zone—again, another suggestion he would ignore. Over the years he had timed exactly how long they would let his car linger before they had it towed. He would have enough time to secure the girl before they took his car.

He sprinted into the airport and slowed to a walk, sucking oxygen. *When did you get so winded, old man?* As a young marine, he had been able to sprint for miles. What happened to that cocky young jarhead? *What didn't,* Leo thought before pushing the thought away. Now wasn't the time to put his life under a microscope. In fact there was never a good time for that, which was why he refused to do it. He was surviving. He'd had enough near misses to appreciate that fact and keep his focus on it, possibly indefinitely. If he pulled back the scope and looked closely at what he'd become, he wasn't certain survival would look like such a benefit anymore.

The girl was already there and waiting on him. He had no trouble finding her because she stuck out as much as he knew she would. In an airport teeming with every manner of person, she was still singular —alone, innocent, small, and slight, her long dark hair secured in a thick braid that trailed down to the middle of her back, a long dress, too homespun to be stylish. He expected her to be either afraid or excited but she was neither, at least as far as he could tell. Her face was a total blank as she stared around her, observing people as if they were the mice and she was the scientist.

"Esther." He tasted the name out loud, priding himself for his remembrance. She looked like an Esther somehow, as if someone shook the old family bible and she fell out.

Her big eyes rested on him, surveying him from the top of his head to the tips of his toes, as if doing a full body scan to pull out and examine more closely at a later time. "Yes," she said at last, as if he'd been waiting on her agreement.

"Ready?" he asked.

"Yes," she said again, same even tone.

He supposed he should make polite conversation, ask her about her trip, about the contest that brought her here, about her life. But he didn't. He couldn't. Long ago he had run out of empty chatter and given up on polite society. Words were a luxury he didn't waste on just anyone. When was the last time he talked, really talked to someone? He couldn't remember, but it didn't matter. She was the job. All that was required of Leo was keeping her safe, and he could do that. Easily, he thought with some bitterness. It was likely why he'd been given the task, because there was no challenge to it. He was fading. He knew it, The Colonel knew it, the entire intelligence community knew it. Burnout hovered over his head like a death cloud. At this moment in time, he didn't much care. Let them fire him; let them kill him. What was it to him? At least then he'd finally get some rest.

They retrieved her luggage and reached his car as it was being hooked to a tow. "No," Leo said, using his foot to kick aside the chain. He held the door for Esther, practically shoving her inside in his haste to take off. In the background, airport security gave him an earful about the lawfulness of parking in a no parking zone. Leo tuned him out, started the car, and zoomed away.

The rain had ended. Leo belatedly realized he was soaked from his dash to the car. He blasted the heat, pointing it at his soggy midsection. Esther uttered a word, her first since "yes."

"What?" he said, unable to hear her over the blast of the heater.

"Petrichor," she repeated, louder this time.

"That some kind of dinosaur?" he asked.

"No, it's the smell of the earth after rain." She inhaled deeply and turned her face to the window.

Okay, he thought but didn't comment. He only knew the vaguest details of her life. She had won some sort of contest to nab her current gig, meaning she was some sort of smarty pants. Geek or no geek, it was nothing to him. She could be the smartest person in the world or the dumbest, he didn't care. She was the job and nothing more.

He inhaled deeply, smelling the smell of renewed earth after a rain. *Petrichor.* Who knew?

*E*sther's father had found the apartment for her. Leo helped her carry her things up three flights. His first sight of her new living arrangement was her first sight, but that was nothing unusual. Esther was used to other people ordering her life for her. Not that she needed or even wanted them to, it was simply how it was in her world. Now apparently the United States government and Leo were in charge of her. So be it.

"I'll pick you up in the morning and drive you to work," Leo said after all her bags had been carried and set inside the tiny space.

"I'd like to be early," she said because he seemed like the kind of guy who was always late, as evidenced by the fact that he was late to pick her up this morning and seemed to be wearing the clothes he slept in last night, if their crumpled state was any indication.

"Something told me you would," Leo replied. It was possible he was making fun of her. Esther didn't know and didn't care. They remained quiet, inspecting each other from twelve inches away, an intimate distance to share with a stranger. Esther supposed he was handsome, in a rugged secret agent sort of way. He wasn't overly tall, not as tall as her father, but he was compact and solidly built, all muscle, like a bull. Or a lion, if his name was any indication. His eyes were a muddy shade of either brown or green and his face was slathered in wiry stubble. Some men tried to grow that sort of stubble to be sexy, Esther knew, but in Leo's case she thought he had merely neglected to shave that day. He probably dated women who wore lots of makeup and skimpy clothes, had probably never met a woman who did puzzles for fun and had made her own butter with cream straight from the cow.

"Do you need anything else before I go?" he asked, hoping desperately she would say no. What if she was that sort who could always find something for a man to do? Something to lift, assemble, or hook up?

"The else in this case is extraneous," she said.

"What?" he asked, blinking at her in confusion.

"You asked what else I might need, but I haven't actually needed anything to begin with, though I do appreciate your assistance," she said.

"Are you a grammar nazi?" he asked.

"No."

"Hmm." They regarded each other in silence again. "I'm going to take off, then, unless you can think of else for me to do."

The corner of her mouth tipped in what might have been a smile but was such a small movement it was hard to discern. "I think your else is safe for now. But keep your phone handy. I tend to think of things that need doing at three in the morning."

"Is this how you tease men, Esther?" he asked.

"Maybe. You won't know for certain until three," she said.

Her delivery was so deadpan it was hard to know if she was teasing or serious. Either way she wasn't like anyone he'd ever encountered, and that said something. As he watched, she turned away from him and stared out the window, summarily dismissing him. Relieved, he slipped out the door, closing and locking it behind him.

CHAPTER 2

Leo was early, but Esther still waited on the street for him, a bag slung over her shoulder, her hands loaded with something he couldn't discern. He wondered if he was supposed to get out and open the door for her. How far did this chauffer gig extend? And how long would it take before it made him weary? He was a highly trained agent, and he had been reduced to shadowing the world's most unwanted woman. Ouch for him and his long and storied career.

She didn't say good morning as she slid into the car, but she did hand him whatever was in her fingers. Bread, as it turned out, slathered thickly with butter. He was still half hung over, but he didn't protest the offering. And it wasn't until he'd polished it off in three bites that he realized how good it was.

"You make that?" he asked.

"Compliments of my grandmother," she said, tossing him the almost smile again.

"Man, if I had access to something that good, I don't think I'd share," he mused.

"What's the point of not sharing? It's only fresh for a couple of days, and I can't eat it all within that time. Hoarding does no one any favors."

"Good point, give me some of your coffee," he commanded. He was teasing her and therefore surprised when she put her travel mug in his hand.

"It's for you. I already ate and drank."

"Thanks. I'm not good with breakfast," he said.

"Something told me you weren't," she said.

"Do others realize you're secretly sassy, or is it too subtle for their notice?" he asked.

"People definitely realize something is different about me," she said, turning to stare out the window.

"Nervous?" he asked.

"I don't get nervous," she said.

She didn't seem nervous, but neither was she the cocky sort. In fact she seemed…flat. Her tone lacked intonation, her face lacked expression. If not for the fact that she'd mildly teased him twice and almost smiled once, he might find her robotic. As it was, he found her soothing, if a bit odd. He would rather have unnatural silence versus incessant chattering, especially when his head pounded. Though, after wolfing down her bread and coffee, his head didn't pound so much. And the silence was so gentle on his nerves he felt downright cheerful as they pulled into the lot.

He paused at the gate while the guard inspected their credentials. He wore civilian clothes, but Leo could tell he was military. Was that his next ignoble landing spot, playing guard to a building full of spies? When he thought about it, maybe the guard had it better. At least his position was respectable. At least he wasn't playing nursemaid to a civilian.

At last the guard waved them through. Leo found parking and faced Esther. "Last chance to back out."

"I said goodbye to the life I left behind," she said.

She seemed sincere in her lack of nerves. Leo seemed to be feeling them on her behalf. She had no idea the world she was about to enter. Clearly she was naïve and innocent, had probably never seen death, probably never met a bad guy in real life. Behind the walls of this building, she would be confronted with all the ugliness in the world.

He swiped a hand wearily over his face. Blast The Colonel for giving him this job that made him feel and think when all he wanted to do was numbly exist.

He lowered his hand and saw Esther watching him, eyes alight with questions she wouldn't voice.

"Let's roll," he snapped, much harsher than he intended. Keeping her safe was one thing. Being in charge of her emotional wellbeing was quite another, a task he lacked the energy, stamina, or desire to do. He expected to see her face crumple like a wounded bunny. It was the female's natural reaction to him, it seemed. But Esther merely turned her stoic eyes to the window as she reached for the handle of her door, and somehow that was worse. But Leo wasn't the sort to apologize, so he didn't. They entered the building in silence, both going through the many layers of security by rote, as if they'd done it a million times before, when in reality this was their first.

Leo pushed the button on the elevator, and the door slid safely closed. "How did you end up here?" he blurted when he couldn't take the silence any longer.

"I like puzzles and patterns. I thought the contest was for a free can of coffee. And then someone called to tell me I'd been recruited." She paused, frowning. "It was all very odd, even for me."

"You didn't have to go through with it," he said, his tone half accusing, half exasperated. Did she even realize what she was in for?

"Did you ever feel like you've been wheeling through life coddiwomple?" she asked.

"Cobby what?"

"Coddiwomple, the feeling of speeding somewhere with no destination in mind. That was my life. At least this is a destination," she said.

"Coddiwomple," he repeated, letting the phrase fill up the oppressive quiet of the elevator. Somehow it did, soaking up the silence like a paper towel on an oil slick. Esther gave a little smile, as if thinking the same thing.

They arrived at the designated floor, and Leo took a breath. There was one part of the job The Colonel warned him about, one thing he dreaded. And it wasn't a what, so much as a who.

The doors opened and Leo came face to face with his old rival and new supervisor, Lieutenant Cameron Ridge.

"Lieutenant," Ridge said, nodding slightly.

"Lieutenant," Leo said, nodding in return. "This is Esther." The introduction was unnecessary. Esther stood between them, big-eyed gaze bouncing back and forth. But somehow Leo felt like he needed to establish dominance where Esther was concerned, in case Ridge got any ideas. Ladies had always gone gaga for his pretty boy features and SEAL pedigree, much to Leo's annoyance. Ridge turned his megawatt smile on Esther.

"Esther, I'm Cameron Ridge. Welcome. Follow me to your cubicle and we'll meet the rest of the team. That's LuAnn." He pointed to a woman with ebony skin, her hair in some sort of twist. Currently she was on the phone and did nothing more than toss them a distracted smile, but it was a nice smile and seemed unfazed when neither Esther nor Leo returned it. "Babs." Ridge pointed to another cubicle where a pretty woman with long dark hair sat typing at a computer. She tossed them a hello. Leo made a mental note to come back to that one later for further inspection. "Ellen." Ellen was middle aged and blond, her hair falling roundly along her chin. She gave them the same smile as her coworkers. "Blue. You'll be working closely with him."

They paused by Blue's cubicle. "Esther and Leo," Blue said with the odd tone of someone who was glad to be adding a face to knowledge he already possessed. In Leo's last assignment, he was imbedded with a group of anarchists in Portland. Blue had all the markings of a hacker, and Leo was instantly suspicious. The good ones were usually not on the side of law and order. And if he was a hacker, he had doubtless peeked into all their personal records. Hackers couldn't help themselves; they were the peeping Toms of the virtual world. Leo regarded him with a cool stare, wishing for his shades. He hated being without them, hated letting other people see his eyes. He wanted to be the observer, not the observed.

"And Maggie," Ridge continued. His tone was different this time, pulling Leo's attention off the hacker and onto the woman in question. She was heavily pregnant, possibly uncomfortable, but she smiled warmly.

"Hi, welcome to the team. We're pleased to have you."

Leo stared, not at her but at Ridge's hand where it rested on her shoulder, his thumb rubbing a slow circle. Lieutenant Cameron Ridge was involved with a coworker, one who was pregnant, no less. The guy was so squeaky clean and by-the-book he could have been a military poster child, back in the day. Was he having an affair with this woman? Was the baby his?

"Maggie's my wife," Ridge added, as if he could sense Leo's shock and judgment.

Of course they were married. Cameron Ridge would never do anything as scandalous as impregnate a random coworker. Still, he had bent his rigid self-control enough to become involved in a relationship with a coworker. Maybe he was human after all.

"You're in your sixth month," Esther said, taking them all by surprise.

"Yes," Maggie said, blinking at her in question.

Esther reached out, laying her hands on Maggie's bump. "A boy," she announced. "He's already in position. He'll come early, quickly, and be over eight pounds."

Maggie blinked at her. "Are you a baby psychic?"

"No, my mother is a midwife."

"Oh, how fascinating," Maggie exclaimed.

"Not really, it's dangerous and a bit archaic. The fact that she hasn't been sued or prosecuted is some kind of anomaly. So much can go wrong when a woman has a baby," Esther replied.

"Oh," Maggie stammered, her face paling slightly. Ridge looked similarly uncomfortable.

"Look, there's our cubicle," Leo said. "Let's go." He took Esther by the elbow and steered her down the hall to the empty office.

"Did I say something wrong?" she asked, her flat affect not revealing any emotion.

"Pregnant women generally don't like hearing all the ways things could wrong," he said. He sat and propped his feet on the table, prepared for a long day of boredom.

"Working here means she's intelligent, and intelligent women know the inherent risks involved with childbirth," Esther said.

"There's knowing something and then there's feeling it," Leo said.

"The feeling part is where people lose me," Esther said. She shrugged out of her oversized cardigan and sat. "Should I go apologize?"

"Nah, that would only make it weirder," he said. "Let's hide out here in our cubicle until they come tell us what we're supposed to be doing."

"Monachopsis," she murmured.

"Who?" he asked, darting his head around her in search of coffee. Had they passed a tray of muffins on the way in, or had that been his imagination?

"Monachopsis, the subtle but persistent feeling of being out of place," Esther said.

"That sums up my entire life," Leo said.

"Same," Esther replied, her eyes roaming the tiny cubicle. She turned on the computer and began arranging the display to her liking. The phone buzzed. Leo answered, momentarily forgetting he wasn't the one who was supposed to answer.

"Blue for you," he said, holding the phone to Esther. She took it and listened a minute before hanging up.

"What did he say?" Leo asked when it became apparent she wouldn't volunteer the information.

"He wants me to look at some information they're working on," she said, clicking open a file in her email.

"Can I look at it?"

She glanced at him over her shoulder. "Why would I care?"

"Some women don't like men to come in and take over."

He thought she laughed, but the sound lacked amusement. "I can't imagine. In any case, suit yourself." She scooted her chair over so he could pull up beside her. Her scent overwhelmed him, shocking in its potency. He inhaled deeply and she glanced at him.

"I've been away from women too long, apparently," he said.

"What?" She stared at him blankly, as if she hadn't noticed the way his nose had tried to suck up all available scent molecules.

She was so…other. It didn't occur to him to be anything less than honest. "You smell incredible."

"Ah. Here." She held out her wrist for his closer inspection, allowing him to take another lingering whiff.

"What is that?" he asked. Whatever it was, he was going to buy it for the next woman in his life and douse her in it like a baptism.

"Vanilla," Esther said and faced forward.

"Vanilla what?"

"Vanilla, actual vanilla. My family buys it in bulk from Haiti."

"It's like sitting next to a sugar cookie," he said, not resisting the urge to inhale again.

"Men are hardwired to enjoy food scents."

She said it with her usual lack of inflection, leaving him to wonder if she purposely wore vanilla to appeal to men. "Is that why you chose it?"

"That would be absurd," she said.

"That wasn't a no," he countered but she ignored him, intent now on reading whatever was on the computer. Even though a moment ago he'd been dead curious about the work, he was now more curious about her. He studied her profile, secure in the knowledge that she was so into her task she had no idea he stared. She was pretty in a wholesome, untouched sort of way. She wore no makeup, had probably never worn makeup, but she also had that sort of milky clean complexion that spoke of proper care and nutrition. Fast food and soft drinks likely hadn't been a part of her life, if the homemade bread was any indication. Her hair was dark, long, and thickly contained in the milkmaid braid. He wondered, all of a sudden, what it would look like let loose and quickly reeled his thoughts back. *Nope.* She was the job, and therefore off limits. But more than that, her virginal wholesomeness put her out of reach. Even after such a short acquaintance he knew they were on opposite ends of the spectrum. Leo had lived hard and fast, shoving as much depravity as he could into his thirty two years. Esther had likely been sheltered from everything he'd done, from his very existence. Somehow the thought made him unaccountably sad, for reasons he couldn't articulate. Maybe because long ago he'd been much closer to the person she was than the person he'd become. So many years on the job, so many emotional wounds had made him calloused, hard, closed off, *other* in a whole different way.

Suddenly Esther stood, jarring him from his morose reverie "What?" he asked, knowing already she wouldn't tell him if he didn't drag it out of her.

"There's a problem."

"What?" he asked again, but she was already out of their cubicle and heading toward Blue, now deep in conversation with the pretty brunette—Babs, was it? *Are they a thing?* Leo wondered but had no time to find out as Esther burst onto the scene, scoring their immediate attention.

"There's a problem," she declared.

"With what?" Blue asked.

"Can you bring up the thing you sent me?" She gestured to his computer the way his grandmother used to gesture at Leo's gun, as if it were a thing beyond her comprehension.

Blue typed, his fingers a blur on the keys, and Esther leaned in. "There. That's the same man."

Blue leaned in, too. "What? No, those are two different people."

"No. It's the same man," Esther said.

Blue stared at the screen. "How are you getting that?"

"See, the structure of the face is the same with slight cosmetic differences," Esther said, tapping the screen.

"But these have been run through facial recognition software purposely designed to recognize facial structure," Blue said.

"If I were going to get cosmetic surgery to change my appearance, I would go for something to fool the software," Esther said. "Can you do an overlay of the skeletal structures?"

"I can do anything," Blue said with so much underlying annoyance Leo wondered if he was the one who wrote the facial recognition software. Secretly, he hoped Esther was right, if for no other reason than she was his responsibility. They were the outsiders here, both of them together. But he wasn't certain she was. He'd been in the spy game a long time, done a lifetime's worth of surveillance. To him, the pictures looked like two separate men, at least until Blue did some sort of computer mojo and laid the images atop each other. He had some sort of software that mapped their features, something that looked like it might be used to reconstruct a face from the skull bones, like with mummies at the museum. Less than thirty seconds after he started the overlay, it beeped with a message: The match was exact.

"Uh-oh," Blue said, reaching for his phone. He pushed a button and spoke again. "We have a problem, and you're going to want to hear about it in person. Right." He stood, suddenly tense. "Come with me." Without waiting for a response, he turned and walked away.

Esther and Leo looked at each other. *"Are we in trouble?"* she mouthed.

"You are," he mouthed in return, miming a halo around his head. The corner of her mouth tipped in the almost smile again. He took her elbow and propelled her after Blue.

CHAPTER 3

They seemed to have no idea what to do with her, no idea what she was capable of. In a world where everything was known, Esther was a question mark. Leo was strangely proud of that, of her, especially after the discovery that blew their ongoing investigation to smithereens, turning it on its ear. They weren't looking for two men; they were looking for the same man playing dress up. That was how he kept evading them, by pretending to be someone else so elaborately they had bought it, hook, line and sinker. The suspect had gone so far as to create a second online persona for himself. Somehow he must have known he was being hacked and watched online. He had counted on the facial recognition software and all the other tech the team could throw at him. What he hadn't counted on was the human element; he hadn't counted on Esther.

If the new job didn't know what to do with her professionally, they had even less idea what to do with her personally. They found her odd, off putting, uncomfortable, never knowing what to make of her alternating cool silences or blurted statements. Leo was used to being an outsider. It was strange to have someone else now inhabiting that space along with him. And it was stranger still how much it bothered him for her sake. She was young, naïve, and clearly sheltered. This seemed to be her first time away from home, first time in a city. Of *course* she was unprepared for socialization, for being a spy. But Leo, who saw more of her than anyone else, knew she was a nice kid, deep down. Maybe it was the daily breakfast and coffee she plied him with, maybe it was because she was his assignment, or maybe it was because they shared their outcast status. Whatever the reason, he was on her side, fully and completely. As far as he was concerned, it was an us-versus-them scenario.

And he knew something else about Esther: she had a crush on him. Perhaps "crush" was the wrong word. She wasn't the type to fawn, flush, and giggle like a schoolgirl. But they spent ten to twelve hours a day together in tight spaces. He had made a study of her expressions, limited as they were, and he understood her feelings ran deeper than professionalism. It was only natural, he supposed. Not that he was a catch by anyone's definition. He'd never had trouble finding a woman, but the quality of woman he usually attracted didn't stick around much longer than the next free meal. So he was especially careful not to do anything to encourage Esther's mislaid crush. She was new, young, and impressionable. In many ways he was her caretaker. It was a classic setup for mislaid admiration. He was certain when something newer and shinier came along, she would forget her feelings for him. In the meantime, he was thankful he didn't return the sentiment. Not that she was wholly unattractive. The raw material was rather pleasant, and he didn't mind looking at her when she was lost in work, as she almost always was. But she was so wholesome, so pure and untouched. It gave him the heebie-jeebies. Women in his world were fast, hard, and experienced, and that was how he preferred them. Esther was like a little rosebud at first frost. She made him feel strangely protective of her innocence, a fact he sort of hated and resented. He was her keeper at work. Did that have to mean he was her keeper in all the other parts of her life? No. He refused. That was why he'd been careful to keep things purely professional, to learn as little about her as possible.

It was growing harder, though. Not because she revealed things about herself, but because, the more time they spent together, the more curious he became.

"Esther, how old are you?" he asked during their second week of work. Currently he stared at the top of her head as they sat across from each other in a conference room. A series of pictures was spread in front of her. Ridge wanted her to look at them and see if she could find any correlation or pattern. They'd already been scanned by a computer but, as they were learning, having a human computer was an added bonus. So far Ridge had been tossing her little bits and pieces of things, trying to figure out how best to employ her unique gifts. To Leo's satisfaction, she hadn't failed at anything, always finding something their precious computer had missed, much to Blue's stupefaction.

"Twenty four," she said without looking up. Absolutely nothing would take her focus off the job until Leo declared it was time for lunch and peeled her away. Then they would eat a hurried lunch in the break room and she would scurry back to the task until it was finished.

He whistled softly. "I have guns older than you."

That earned a look. She peered up at him, squinting, trying to read him the way she read her puzzles and pictures. What bugged Leo was how often she succeeded. "You don't strike me as a collector."

"I'm not, but I enjoy them. Maybe someday when I'm old and have time and money."

She was still doing the narrow eyed gaze. "If you don't begin making yourself what you want to be now, you won't succeed in doing it when you're older. Age isn't a magic formula for achievement and intelligence."

He blinked at her. "Wow, that was some kind of deep wisdom."

"I've got a million of them," she said, her tone deadpan as she dropped her head and returned to her work.

He studied the top of her head some more, strangely averse to the end of conversation. Perhaps it was boredom. For the last few weeks, he had done nothing but sit and watch her work. The inactivity was killing him. How long was he going to be an overpaid, underworked babysitter? He had tried asking The Colonel and gotten a grunt in return, meaning The Colonel probably had no idea, meaning his life was now at the whim of whichever bureaucrat thought it would be a super neat fantastic idea to bring on a civilian with no training, based on her ability to solve a puzzle.

"Give me a word," he demanded. Esther, he discovered, was a logophile, a lover and collector of words. Leo had come to enjoy the words, too. It was like having a human word of the day calendar at his fingertips.

"Zemblanity."

"What's it mean?" he asked.

She made a little shooing motion with her fingers. Sighing, he reached for his phone and looked it up. Zemblanity: an unhappy surprise or discovery, the opposite of serendipity.

"Well, that's depressing," he said.

She glanced quickly up, bestowing one of her half-quirked smiles. Unconsciously, he reached out and began drumming his fingers on the table. Esther's hand reached over and flattened them. She didn't like repetitive little noises, couldn't stand them, in fact.

"I'm bored," he declared.

She moved aside and patted the space beside her. Relieved, he angled his chair beside her, turned it around, and straddled it as he sat backwards, leaning over to inspect the pictures before him. They were a series of executions, gruesome in the extreme. He had the sudden thought that she shouldn't be seeing these and turned to inspect her instead.

"These don't bother you?" he asked.

She didn't answer. He faced forward again, frowning, resisting the urge to gather the photos, stalk down the hall, and shove them in Cameron Ridge's face. Why would he foist such gruesome photos on such an innocent kid? It was wrong and gross. If it were anyone else, Leo might wonder if he was purposely trying to drive Esther away. But, much as they didn't get along, Ridge had never been the type to fight dirty. He was too squeaky clean for that. His by-the-book rule following nature was one of the reasons he annoyed Leo so much. Opposites in every way, oil and water, the two of them were.

"We could ask them to put you on something else," Leo said.

"Leo," she replied, not looking up.

"What?" he asked.

"Please." She touched her finger to his, softening the word. She couldn't stand extraneous noise while she worked, the reason they were in the conference room. The cubicle was too noisy for her to concentrate. That was how Leo knew she had a crush on him, because she allowed him to accompany her to the work room instead of remain in the cubicle, banished and waiting. "There." She sat back and rubbed her eyes.

"What? Where?" He looked at the pictures, a dozen scenes of death that seemingly had nothing in common, minus the fact that all the subjects were corpses.

"These five were done by the same hand." She tapped five pictures. Leo leaned in for closer inspection.

"What am I missing?" The pictures looked nothing alike to him; the manner of death wasn't even the same.

"It's the tilt of the head. They're positioned the same way. And in these two the, ah, skin flap has the same signature." She was no longer looking at the pictures. Instead she sat back, head tilted away.

"Esther, are you okay?" he asked.

She nodded. "We should get this information to Ridge."

"Hmm." He regarded her as he reached for his phone, firing off a short text. Ridge arrived a short time later, Ethan at his side. Ethan wasn't usually in the office, only popped in occasionally. Leo breathed a sigh of relief. Ethan was more his style, much more relaxed than their uptight boss. With him there as a buffer, the meeting would undoubtedly go better.

"Esther found something," Leo supplied. Somehow he had become the spokesperson in this weird little scenario. He didn't like it, but he saw no way around it. Esther was clearly uncomfortable with new people, men especially. She tended to blurt things worse if she tried to talk to them directly. Leo knew they saw her as an oddity, perhaps even as a freak, someone to do unusual work and remain silent. It bothered him that they didn't see what he saw. She was quirky, yes, but sweet and thoughtful, kind and funny.

"Sweet," Ethan said, plopping into a chair and propping his feet. "Watcha got?"

Esther glanced at Leo before answering. He gave her an encouraging nod. She cleared her throat. "These five were done by the same person."

Ridge and Ethan leaned in to make their inspection. Ridge's expression was serious, imperative. Ethan's was interested, fascinated. Ridge reshuffled the pictures, putting the five together, pushing aside the other seven. "How certain are you, Esther?"

"If she wasn't certain, I wouldn't have called you," Leo said, resentful on her behalf.

Ridge tossed him an annoyed look before quickly smoothing it away. Leo took more than a little satisfaction in that look. It was always so fun to ruffle the unruffleable. "Lives depend on this information. It has to be infallible," Ridge said tightly.

Everyone turned to survey Esther while Leo edged protectively closer. "I'm certain," Esther decreed.

Ridge gave a little nod and made eye contact with Ethan. "Strike team?" Ethan asked.

"Strike team," Ridge agreed.

Ethan stood and ghosted from the room, already in stealth mode. Or maybe he was in it so often he couldn't turn it off now. Leo itched to go with him, to join the action, to remove the threat. His hands flexed and he rubbed his palms together. He'd been in a lot of lousy situations over the years, but playing nursemaid might actually break him.

"Thank you, Esther. I appreciate this. You've saved a lot of lives today," Ridge said. Grudgingly, Leo admitted it was decent of him to thank her, something he likely didn't do for everyone. Perhaps it was a sign that he realized how untouched she was.

Esther gave a little nod. "Excuse me. I'm going to," she pointed out

the door, toward the restroom and disappeared, almost as silently as
Ethan, leaving Leo and Ridge in awkward silence.

"How's she doing?" Ridge asked. Since she was clearly doing well at
the job, Leo understood it was a question about her emotional wellbeing.

"It's hard to tell. She's untouched and self-contained," Leo said.

Ridge nodded. He glanced at the door and took a breath, as if
gearing up for something difficult. "We're on the same side here, Leo.
I care about my team, all of them. The past, it's that: the past. As far as
I'm concerned, you and I have a clean slate."

"I'm not certain I can say the same, but I'll try. Esther is the job and
therefore my priority. Anything personal doesn't get in the way." He
wanted to mean it, but theirs was a murky history.

Ridge nodded and let himself out of the room. Leo waited a couple
of beats and left as well, letting himself into the women's bathroom
without knocking.

As he suspected, Esther was in a stall, heaving into a commode,
pale and sweating. He wet a paper towel and applied it to her forehead, laying his palm reassuringly in the center of her back. After a
few shaky breaths, she stood and leaned hard on the side of the stall,
resting her cheek against the cool metal.

"Which is worse, seeing men who've already been killed or
knowing lives now rest on your work?" he asked.

"Dead men," she whispered, face and lips pale. "My work is solid."

He laughed, earning the half smile from her. "Cockiness is important in this world, kid. I think you're going to do just fine." Even so he
put out his arm and pulled her against him, letting her lean on his
chest instead of the wall. She did so, leaning into him without
embracing him in return, as he somehow knew she would.

"Thanks."

"My job," he said.

She pulled away and peered up at him, big eyes serious. "I know. I
know this is a job to you, Leo, that I'm a job to you. I don't delude
myself. But I'm still ridiculously grateful. I don't know what I'd do
without you, what I'll do without you when your part in this is over."

She bit her lip, the first sign of worry or nerves he'd ever witnessed from her.

"Then let's make sure and get you ready to stand on your own," Leo said. "You're smart and capable, Es. Just a little untested. You'll get there. Everyone starts somewhere."

She nodded, believing him completely, merely because he was the one who said it. Had anyone ever had that much faith in him? It was unnerving because there was nowhere to go but down. In Leo's experience it was usually better to start at the bottom and work his way up, to take people by surprise rather than let them down. He felt the viselike grip of panic edge up his throat. "Let's get out of here. You've been working like crazy. We'll go out for lunch today, okay?"

"I packed lunch for us," she said.

He rolled his eyes. "Of course you did." She packed lunch for them every day, and brought him breakfast and coffee in the mornings. He had probably gained five pounds in the last two weeks, but it was weight he needed. He had become too rangy after too many missed meals and too many liquid lunches. His brain felt sharper after so much sustenance, his body less sore. Another couple of weeks under her careful ministration and he'd be back in fighting shape. "Bring it and we'll have a picnic in the park."

"Okay," she said, cheeks flushing with pleasure. He wanted to warn her away from him, to tell her to hurry up and get over her crush already. He wasn't worth it, would let her down and hurt her, sooner rather than later. On the other hand, it was nice to be someone's hero for once.

"Esther."

"Hmm?" She was doing the doe-eyed thing again, twisting her long braid between her fingers.

He reached in his pocket and withdrew a tin of Altoids. "Have a mint. Your breath smells like puke."

"I guess you'd know," she said, accepting the proffered mint.

He was hung over nearly every Monday, something he didn't think she realized but apparently did. "Is that why you bring me food?"

"Among other reasons," she said, popping the mint between her lips.

"What reasons?" he asked.

She shook her head.

"For a puritan, you're kind of a mystery," he noted.

"For a spy, you're kind of transparent," she returned.

"Okay, let's get you out of this office. The sass is apparently seeping into your brain." Clasping her hand, he led her out of the bathroom.

CHAPTER 4

Getting out of the office was easier said than done. Leo was suspicious Maggie Ridge gave everyone some sort of talk saying, "Reach out to the new people," because absolutely everyone stopped them on their way toward the door. From what he'd observed, Ridge might be in charge of work at the office but Maggie was in charge of the office's social life, at least unofficially. They'd only been on the job for a few weeks but already there had been cake, cookies, and muffins on tap.

Babs was the last to say goodbye. With effort, Leo tamped down his disappointment. She was the type of woman who usually fell for guys like him; he had a sense about these things and therefore had high hopes for her. But, alas, she was involved with Maggie's brother, if the rumors were true. *There are other people in the world,* he wanted to tell them. *Your lives don't have to be so interconnected with your coworkers.* On the other hand, he got it. Theirs was a strange world, often plunging them into tight quarters, dangerous situations, adrenaline highs and lows. Relationships tended to go deeper, resentments to fester longer.

At last they broke free of the office and drove to a nearby park. It was a sunny spring day, unexpectedly warm for so early in the season.

Leo had no blanket to spread, because of course he wasn't the type of man who kept a picnic blanket in his car, but Esther didn't seem to mind, as he knew she wouldn't. She took off her shoes, tossed them aside, and spread her toes in the grass.

He assumed she grew up on a farm. She had the type of fresh-faced wholesomeness that could only be earned by fresh air, hard work, and feet and hands in the soil. He hadn't asked. There was a line of demarcation between them, one he tried hard never to cross. She was the job and only the job. Learning personal facts about her might blur the line he tried hard to maintain.

They ate in comfortable silence, both watching the people around them in different ways. Leo was wary. After so many years in the military and espionage, he never fully trusted public spaces. He tended to mark the exits and assess the threat wherever he went and outside in a park was no exception. The people around them seemed to be like them—office dwellers in search of a reprieve. But he hadn't stayed alive to the ripe age of thirty two by letting down his guard.

Esther liked to observe people, even if she didn't engage with them easily. It was as if she had been sent from another planet to examine life on earth and learn the wheres and whys of humanity. He thought she was absorbed in staring at strangers, so it came as something of surprise when she spoke to him.

"Leo, can I ask you a question?"

"Fire away," he said. Having determined there were no immediate threats in the area, he rolled onto his back and stared up at her, noting the way her fingers twisted idly though the end of her braid. He was momentarily distracted, wondering what it looked like loose, how much longer it would be. It must be immensely thick; the braid alone was almost the width of his hand.

"The first day we arrived, you called Ridge Lieutenant."

"He was a Lieutenant Commander in the navy, the head of some elite SEAL squad."

"It's my understanding all SEAL teams are elite," she said.

"Don't try to provoke me on such a sunny day," he said, closing his eyes against the sun's glare. She knew he was a marine, knew the two branches were rivals. That much about his past he'd told her.

"You may have noticed there was no question in those statements. My question is this: why did he call you lieutenant in return?"

Leo sighed. He didn't want to get into it, the whole sordid story. On the other hand, it was better that she hear it from him than someone else. "I was a Second Lieutenant in the corps."

"Is that how you two knew each other? Do all lieutenants know each other?" she asked.

He laughed and opened his eyes. "No, but the world of military intelligence is fairly small. Ridge and I crossed paths a few times. And there was this woman."

"Isn't there always?" she asked.

He laughed again. "In my experience, yes." He thought of Cassie. She'd been different from the others, good, decent. Leo had sensed the difference and been attracted to it for reasons he couldn't articulate. He and Ridge had both pursued her. She chose Ridge. That had been aggravating. What was worse was that they broke up a month later, had never even been serious. It was one thing to lose out to a man if it ended up being a lifetime commitment and another entirely to lose out to a halfhearted fling. Leo had liked Cassie, really liked her. They'd been friends. After the breakup with Ridge, she called and texted, but he'd lost his heart for the game, for the chase. In that instance, being second best hurt too much.

"Is that why you don't like him?" she asked. "Because of the girl?"

"That's one of the reasons," he said. He had closed his eyes again. He sensed her watching him and opened them again, staring up at her as she stared down at him in question. "You really want to know why?"

She nodded. "He's my boss and you're my handler. Seems like I should understand the animosity between you."

"I'm not sure I could explain it in a way you'd understand. Was there ever a girl in your school you didn't get along with?"

"I was homeschooled," she said.

"Right, right," he said. He swiped a hand over his face and sat up.

"As I said, our paths crossed a few times and he was always golden, you know what I mean? Our superiors practically worshiped him, as did his team. His missions always went according to plan and succeeded. Meanwhile I couldn't seem to get along with anyone." He paused. "I was kind of waiting for you to jump in with some disbelief."

She released a puff of air that might have been a laugh. "I suggest you stop waiting."

He poked her. "Anyway, he was the golden boy, he got the girl, and then…"

"And then what?" she prodded, her somber tone now matching his.

"There was a mission that didn't go as planned. Sometimes they don't. We lost a few men. Some people said it was my fault. I didn't listen, didn't follow orders, wanted to do it on my own, make a name, be the hotshot."

"Is any of that true?" she asked.

"Honestly? I don't know. I was younger, cockier, more full of myself than I am now."

"Now is when I'm going to jump in with my disbelief."

It was so unexpected that he laughed and lay back down again. "The official inquiry said it wasn't my fault, and I'm still here. I doubt The Colonel would have kept me on the payroll if he thought I was to blame."

"But you still blame yourself," she said, more gently than he'd ever heard her.

He paused, his throat and chest tightening painfully. "Yes." Being a marine was the thing that was supposed to save him. He'd left his painful childhood and thrown himself into the job. When the job went bad, he had nowhere else to go and he began to wonder if it wasn't the circumstances of his life that made it bad. Maybe it was him; maybe he really was a perpetual screwup.

Her hand reached out and rested on his chest, flattening like a comfortable weight on his sternum. "Liberosis."

He opened his eyes. "Are you going to make me look that one up?"

"It's the desire to care less about things, to want to let them go."

The description perfectly fit the way he felt. He so badly wanted to let go of the old pain, self-doubt, guilt and recrimination. Drowning it in whiskey hadn't helped; running away from people and the world hadn't done a thing. What would make the old ache go away? Unconsciously, his hand covered Esther's, his thumb smoothing over her fingers. Would she one day end up like him? Trying to find her own escape from the pain?

"Esther, you should go back home and leave this world," he said. "It has to be better there than it is here."

Her big eyes studied him, weighing her next words. "There are different kinds of pain, Leo."

What kind of pain had she experienced at home? He wondered but wouldn't ask. Already they'd veered too far into the personal. She was the job, nothing more. She closed her eyes and tipped her face to the sun, soaking it in.

"Ataraxia," she murmured.

"What is that one?" he asked, but she didn't answer. Later, he pulled out his phone and looked it up. Ataraxia: a state of freedom from emotional disturbance and anxiety; tranquility.

He wondered, then, if Esther said these words to define her own emotions or his because, at the moment she said it, it was what he felt. And then a new possibility occurred: maybe the words described them both.

CHAPTER 5

taraxia lasted for two weeks, two weeks in which Leo thought maybe his mind had finally snapped because the word kept replaying in his head. All he knew was that finding the perfect word to describe the feeling taking place inside him helped somehow, like releasing a pressure valve. He supposed this was why people went to therapy, something he had never ascribed to, to try and put words to the difficult feelings inside them. Maybe Esther would eventually find words for his traumatic childhood, lousy dating history, and cumulative work stress.

For two weeks they functioned as if they were a natural and normal part of the office. Esther worked on whatever odd project Ridge assigned to her, usually attempting to find a pattern or clue where a computer had failed. Leo hovered on the periphery, irritated to be out of the game, fascinated by her ability to see the invisible. Being a paramilitary organization, it didn't take long for people to assign them a nickname—Sherlock and Watson. Leo was beyond chagrined to be the Watson. In his world he had never been the sidekick before, but perhaps that was why he had never played well with others—because he always insisted on being the star. Now that he had no choice in the matter, he realized it wasn't so bad. And it wasn't as if he brought nothing to the table. Esther couldn't drive, was horrible at navigation, never had any idea where they were, and still had only warmed up to her coworkers the most incremental amount. By now everyone had decided to make allowances for her. Babs confessed to him one day it wasn't so different from when they met Jane, Blue's soon-to-be wife. *She has social anxiety, too,* Babs said furtively while Esther was in the bathroom.

Leo was glad they were using lenience for her quirks, but he had his doubts about social anxiety being the root cause of her issues. She wasn't nervous, wasn't shy, had no trouble speaking her mind when provoked. Rather it was more like she lacked a filter entirely, had no ability to temper her words to spare the hearer's feelings. And yet, despite her inability to stop the words from coming, she was astute enough to realize the things she said weren't correct. Leo, who spent more time with Esther than anyone, realized her heart was in the right place, even if her words weren't. In time he hoped everyone else would realize it, too. And then he would be off the hook and able to move on to another assignment.

He was in good shape to transition away from her, so of course he had to screw it up.

He didn't mean to get tanked, but then he never did. One drink turned into another and another. He told himself he had it under control, and then it was nine in the morning and someone pounded on his door.

He roused slowly, and then all at once. Esther. The job. Worse, *The Colonel.* It had finally happened; he had messed up so badly the man showed up at his house. What were the chances he could escape, could move away and start a new life? Not good; The Colonel had contacts in every country.

With dread, Leo wrenched himself from bed and stumbled to the door. He closed his eyes, took a painful breath, and opened the door.

"Esther." She stood on the other side of the door, holding breakfast and coffee like any normal day.

"Leo," she said. "May I come in?"

She remained on the doorstep, awaiting an answer. "Esther."

"Leo."

"How did you get here?"

"I called a taxi."

"You called a taxi."

"Yes, it was quite expensive."

"You took a taxi to my house."

"Yes."

"How did you know where I live?"

"I know where everyone at work lives. I memorized the personnel files one day when I was bored."

"You…mem…what else was in them?" he asked.

"Your social security number, military ID number, birthdate, height, weight, SAT score, college transcripts, and a bunch of notes written by former superiors. I didn't read those, seemed too personal."

"Right, you wouldn't want to cross any boundaries," he said, motioning to the empty hallway outside his apartment.

"Was that sarcasm?"

"Yes, Esther, that was sarcasm, big, fat sarcasm."

She blinked at him. Sarcasm was beyond her reach; Leo had been careful not to use it. "Do you want me to go? I could find another taxi."

He sighed. "No, I don't want you to go, Esther. I want…" *I want a redo on this day, on this life. I want to not be the guy who messes everything up.* He scrubbed his face. "Ridge is going to love this."

"How would he find out?" she asked.

"Because we're not at work," he said.

"I called and told him I would be late," she said.

"You…call…when did you do that?"

"When you were late and didn't answer your phone."

"Huh." He held up his arm. She ducked under and slid inside, holding out breakfast and coffee to him like an offering. He took them and sat at his table, such as it was, a broken heap he picked up eons ago. At least he had two chairs. Esther took the other seat uninvited and rested her face in her hands, staring at him while he chewed. He should probably be embarrassed about, well, everything. His life, his failure, his hovel apartment, his unwashed, hungover body. But there was no judgment in her gaze as she assessed him. Her expression was as blank as usual.

"Why did you come?" he asked after he polished off the exquisite coffee cake, his favorite, and tankard of coffee, made exactly as he liked it with lots of cream and sugar. As usual after she fed him, his head pounded slightly less, the day seemed less glum.

"You're my keeper, Watson."

He grimaced. "I thought maybe you weren't aware of the nickname."

"I'm aware of everything, Leo."

"That you are," he said, closing his eyes against the glare of the overhead light. Esther stood and turned it off.

"It doesn't fit, though. Sherlock was the addict."

"I'm not an addict," he said, his tone more snappish than he'd ever used with her. She didn't respond and the flat expression didn't change. He sighed. "Yeah, okay, I'm an addict. But it's under control, mostly, usually. Last night was a blip."

"Do you want to talk about it?"

His first inclination was to say no, but he remembered how much better he felt after she gave him a word. He craved release, the sort of vent those little sparks of connection gave him. "Yesterday was my father's birthday."

"Your father is dead," she blurted. That information was in his personnel file, of course.

"As a doornail, thankfully. My father was...not a good man." Which had been worse, the abuse or the neglect? Some of Leo's earliest memories were of the pain his father inflicted. And then he left, disappearing as if he'd never existed, until Leo became a marine. Then he entered again, sick and decrepit, wanting absolution. Leo hadn't given it. To this day he didn't know if that was the right or wrong decision. Esther reached out and took his hand, holding on tight. "Give me a word, Esther."

"Hamartia."

"What does it mean?" he rasped, grasping her hand as if it were a lifeline. Maybe it was. No one else had ever sought him out, fed him, listened to his story.

"A flaw that causes the downfall of a hero," she said.

The word was a double-edged sword. His father had been his hero because as much as Leo despised him, he also adored him. Or did she refer to him and his great and many flaws?

"Nepenthe," she said, touching a finger to an empty whiskey bottle. "A tonic used to try and take away the pain." She let go his hand and cupped his face. "Cingulomania."

"What does that one mean?" he whispered, her face too close to his. He should back away, reassert their boundaries. But before he could act, she let him go and stood, turning her back to him as she began to clear the empty bottles from his counter.

"Go take your shower, Leo."

"Don't clean," he said, standing.

"Of course I will," she replied, her tone lacking inflection as usual.

He rolled his eyes at the back of her head. Cleaning was another step, another link between them. It was so…intimate.

"I saw that," she said, tossing a handful of bottles and cans into the garbage.

"Of course you did," he replied. He grabbed his phone and locked the door of the bathroom, leaning on it as he swiped his thumb over the device. It was nearly dead, had only enough battery to look up the word. *Cingulomania: a strong desire to hold another person in one's arms.*

He set his phone down, turned on the water, and stepped beneath the spray.

CHAPTER 6

They didn't speak of the day again. After Leo's shower, they drove to work like usual, if a few hours late. Either Ridge bought Esther's excuse or he didn't call them on it. Whatever the reason, life went on as if nothing happened and Leo vowed, once again, to stop drinking during the week. He had never been the type of guy who had to drink every day. Rather he was the type who, once he started, couldn't seem to stop, an all-or-nothing binger.

Usually when he gave in he only let himself down. But now there was Esther. She depended on him for all the day-to-day things. He felt bad that she'd been left standing on the street waiting for him, felt awful she'd taken a taxi to his apartment to check on his wellbeing, felt worse she found him in such a sorry state and cleaned his apartment while he tried to put himself back together. For the time being, they were partners. When was the last time someone counted on him completely, depended on him for her wellbeing? Had anyone ever? Not that he could recall. He assumed he would find the weight of responsibility crushing, but as the days wore on, he instead felt more tethered, less expendable. With that connection came a waning desire to lose himself in drink.

When they arrived at work a week later, they couldn't help but note the party atmosphere. Chocolate muffins were in the break room and everyone was laughing. "Bonhomie," Esther whispered to Leo who nodded even though he only had a vague idea what the word meant. The atmosphere was festive, more so than usual, and then they figured it out as Babs and Blue hung a giant banner behind the muffins.

"The baby shower," Leo whispered to Esther.

"The baby shower," she echoed, also in a whisper. Out loud she spoke to Babs and Blue. "Excuse me, I forgot what time the party is today. Can you remind me?"

"After lunch," Babs said, humming merrily while she stood on a chair to hang her half the banner. Given the fact that Blue was several inches taller, the banner was predictably crooked. Esther opened her mouth to tell her, but Leo put a hand on her bicep, shaking his head. Apparently people didn't like to be told things that, to Esther, were obvious and helpful. She didn't get it, but she was willing to follow his lead, mostly because he had never steered her wrong and she trusted his judgment on social matters. He liked to pretend he was an outlier, but people liked him, she could tell.

He took her elbow and shepherded her down the hall to their cubicle. "The baby shower," he hissed. "How could we forget?"

"I don't know, but I'm inclined to blame you. You know I'm not so great with social engagements," she said.

"Oh, yeah, my social calendar is filled to the brim with parties and teas," he said, plopping into his chair and resting his feet on the table.

"Is it?" she asked.

"Sarcasm, Esther," he said.

"Big, fat sarcasm," she agreed, nodding.

"There's really no other kind," he said, grinning. "What are we going to do?"

"We could give her money," Esther said.

"She and her husband both make more than we do," he said. "Besides, it's Maggie. She likes the personal touch."

Esther grimaced. "You think we should touch her?"

"That was not a literal suggestion. I meant the gift should be personal," he said.

"It probably goes without saying I'm not great at personal and thoughtful gift buying," she said.

"I've never bought a gift for a baby in my life, but this is going to be an exception. We'll go out at lunch and buy something. How much money do you have?"

She put her purse on the table and dumped it, sorting through the tidy stack until she reached her wallet. She opened it and withdrew the largest stack of money he'd ever seen in real life. "Six thousand dollars."

He stared, first at the money and then at her uncomprehending features. "Esther."

She jumped at his harsh tone. "What?"

"Why are you carrying that much money?"

"For emergencies," she said.

"What sort of emergency would require six thousand dollars in cash?"

She thought about that. "Car repair."

"You don't own a car."

"I don't know. My family carries cash, I guess."

"What about credit cards?" he asked. "You could use your card for an emergency then pay it off."

"I've never had one," she said.

"You've never had a credit card," he said, dumbfounded.

"No, why, have you?"

"Yes, of course. Okay, we're getting you a credit card, and you're going to stop carrying enormous amounts of money on you, thereby making yourself even more of a target."

"What do you mean by more of a target? Why would I be a target in the first place?"

"Because you're a woman."

"Why does being a woman make me a target?"

"Because bad guys are predators looking for easy prey."

"I'm prey?"

He took in her small frame and guileless features "You're chum in the water." He stuffed her money back in her wallet and pushed it into her fingers, watching while she rearranged the items tidily in her purse.

"But I'm always with you, and you are not prey," she said.

"No, but I won't always be with you."

She frowned.

He sighed and leaned forward. "Esther, surely you know this arrangement isn't sustainable. The point of my presence isn't to be your bodyguard forever. It's to get you ready to stand on your own."

He expected argument. Instead she took out a piece of paper and pen. "What do I need to do in order to get ready?"

"You need to get a credit card and stop carrying so much money. You need to get a Metro card and figure out the system. You need to learn DC better so you always know where you are. You need to learn some self-defense in case someone attacks you. You should get a gun and learn how to use it."

"I know how to use guns," she interjected.

Growing up on a farm, he supposed she would be familiar. "Shotgun, rifle, or handgun?" he asked.

She blinked at him. He sighed again and tapped the paper. "Learn to use a hand gun. Put that on the list."

She sat back and studied the list. "That's it? I need to learn to shoot, punch, and navigate?"

No. She needed to become streetwise, to stop looking like a snack for a sex predator, to learn how to talk to people without revealing her complete naiveté, to reach out and connect with people outside their office, to have more situational awareness instead of being lost in her own head all the time, to toughen up, be less vulnerable, be more...

"Let's start with the bank and go from there," he said.

"What about you?" she asked.

"What about me?" he said.

"What do we need to do to transfer you out of this arrangement?" she asked.

He laughed. "Babe, I'm not the one who needs a keeper."

"Aren't you, Leo?" she asked in her steady, expressionless way, and Leo fought the desire to squirm.

"I've been functioning on my own for a long time," he said.

"Not well."

"It's not about me," he said.

"Isn't it? Did it ever occur to you this arrangement was for your benefit as much as mine?" she asked.

"No, it's a punishment." It was the sort of thing which, said to any other woman, would have caused offense. Esther didn't even flinch.

"Is it? Or is it possible your boss thought this might be beneficial for you?"

"How would playing nursemaid to a civilian be beneficial to me?" he asked testily. That was one of the things he liked best about Esther. She might not have a lot of sensitivity toward others, but she wasn't sensitive toward herself, either. He didn't have to temper his words or tiptoe. He could be himself; he could be *real*, and it was an unmitigated relief.

"I only know the barest details of your life, but even I can see you've been running from it, trying to stay active so you don't have to deal with the painful things that have happened. Maybe this time of inactivity is a chance to take a breath, to sit still, to *deal*."

"I don't want to deal," he snapped.

She gave him one of her rare smiles. "I don't want to get a credit card. I don't want to ride the Metro. I don't want to do this without you. But apparently I have to. So man up, Leo, and face your demons."

"I'm not sure I like you right now," he said peevishly.

She glanced away, staring toward the door. "You and everyone else."

"Esther." He dropped his feet from the table, scooted closer, and embraced her, squeezing tight. "You know I'm lying. I like you."

She nuzzled, burrowing her nose against his neck. Esther was a nuzzler; he had not expected that. She seemed more likely to push him off and break away. Instead she leaned in and nestled her nose against the hollow of his throat. She was warm and soft and smelled like vanilla and they were enclosed in a four-foot cubicle where they'd been the last few weeks with little to no outside contact.

"Leo," she whispered.

"What?" he asked, throat scratchy and dry.

She pulled back to see his face, still impossibly close. "How do you know which credit card to get? There are so many. The options are endless."

"It depends on the features," he whispered.

"There are features?" she said, perking up.

"So many features, Es," he said, brushing a finger on her face. He reached for his phone. "You work. Let Watson sort your credit."

"Maybe we should switch that. I've seen your credit score," she said.

"At least I have one," he returned.

She gave a puff of laughter. "Touché." She eased away from him and turned on her computer. He did not miss her warmth and scent. He told himself so repeatedly until he started to believe it.

They took a walking lunch and went shopping, trading off bits of food as they strolled. Leo had never once brought food to her, it was always the opposite. Every day she brought his breakfast and lunch.

"Why do you feed me every day?" he asked, finishing a massive roast beef sandwich, his favorite of all the things she prepared.

"Quid pro quo. You bring the security, I bring the food," she said. "Here we are." They ducked inside a baby shop and felt immediately overwhelmed and out of place.

"How are we supposed to know what to get?" he whispered.

"Ask the saleslady," she whispered.

"You ask the saleslady. It's weird for a guy," he returned.

"She's a saleslady. Charm her." She elbowed him.

He couldn't reply because the saleslady barreled toward them now, the light of a future sale in her eyes. "Hi, can I help you find something?"

"Yes, please," Leo said, giving her his best smile. "We're a little over our heads here."

She glanced between them, "Aw, I know how that goes. When are you due?"

"You think I'm pregnant?" Esther blurted. "With Leo's baby?"

The saleslady's cheeks flushed crimson and her lashes fluttered. "No, um, I, er, it's…a lot of couples come in and…"

Leo decided to save them all. "We're looking for a gift for a coworker."

"How far along is she?" the clerk asked, practically swooning with relief.

"Uh, near the end."

"Is she having a girl or a boy?"

"Boy," they answered together.

"All right, follow me, I'll show you some options."

They found the perfect gift, in Leo's opinion. And if it was so obviously perfect to someone usually oblivious to such things, it must be actually be perfect.

"But why is there writing on an outfit when babies can't read?" Esther asked. They stood at the counter while the clerk wrapped the gift for them.

"Because Maggie's a librarian." The clerk had led them to a selection of clothes with pictures of classic books on them. To Leo, it felt providential.

"Because she's a librarian her baby should have clothes with books on them?" Esther said.

"Yes," Leo said.

"Why?"

"Because it's funny," he said.

"Why?"

"Because…I don't know, Esther. Moms like to dress their kids in stuff that makes them laugh, I guess."

"Shouldn't we be buying something for the baby to enjoy and not his mom?" Esther asked.

"What would that be?" Leo countered.

"Hmm. I see your point. Babies seemingly only care about round the clock nursing. Not much we can do to provide that," Esther said. "I wonder if Maggie will nurse."

"Don't ask," he said.

"Why? Maybe she's not aware of the benefits, though as a librarian…"

"Really don't ask," the salesclerk inserted. "Believe me, I work with a lot of moms. It is not a question they want to receive from non-mothers."

"If I were having a child, I would want to hear differing opinions on the best possible options," Esther said.

"That's what makes you one in a million, Holmes," Leo said, scrolling his phone to pass the time. The clerk smiled benignly at them.

"He's single, in case you were wondering," Esther volunteered.

"Esther," Leo said, glancing up sharply.

"What? You are. And you haven't had a date since we started working together."

"That you know of," he said.

"I can read you, Leo. You've been solitary for too long. This girl is cute, and if the way she's ogling you is any indication, seems into you. Why don't you get her number?"

"Esther, stop it," Leo said.

"But…"

He held up his hand like a stop sign. She pressed her lips together.

"Fine, but I'm eating the last cookie," she declared, reaching for the bag.

"No food in the store, sorry," the rosy cheeked clerk said.

Sighing, Esther turned and walked outside, leaving Leo to wait for their package. "Sorry about that," he added to the clerk.

"It's fine, my cousin's autistic, so I'm sort of used to it."

He stood up straight, his phone going slack. "You think Esther is autistic?"

"Isn't she?"

His eyes slid to the street where Esther presumably stood. "I thought autism was like retardation or people couldn't talk."

"There's a spectrum," the clerk said. She plumped the bow one final time and handed the package to Leo. "There you go." The way she smiled hopefully at him made him realize Esther was once again correct—if not tactful—and the girl was into him. She was cute and sunny and seemed sweet enough, but he couldn't seem to make himself interested enough to engage and ask for her number. Instead he felt a sad sort of malaise—Esther's word from yesterday.

"Thank you," he said.

"Any time. Good luck with your friend." Her glance slid toward the street.

"She's not…" He stopped speaking and tucked the package under his arm. As much as he had wanted to keep Esther as the job and only the job, she had sneaked past his defenses. He might as well admit he cared about her and they were, in fact, friends. Despite all of her blurting and complete lack of filter, she was one of the kindest, warmest, most genuine people he knew. There were no games with her. She said what she meant, always. It was refreshing, if a bit awkward at times.

"Are you mad at me?" she asked when he poked his head outside the shop, package in hand.

"Furious," he said.

Her face fell. "I'm sorry. I was trying to help, really. Matchmaking is clearly not my strong suit."

"I'm joking." He put his arm around her shoulders and gave them a squeeze. "I'm not mad."

"Did you at least get her number?" she asked.

"No. Why did you want me to?" he asked. As far as he knew, she was the one with an inappropriate crush on him. Why was she trying to pawn him off on others?

"You have your list, Leo. I have mine. If you're determined to have done with me, you don't leave me much time to try and fix you." She linked her arm with his, surprising him again. She wasn't one for extraneous touch.

He wanted to ask her about the autism, but before he could try, a car crept into his peripheral vision and sped past them.

"What's wrong?" Esther asked, making Leo realize he'd tensed.

"I saw that car earlier," he said.

"The tan sedan? Yes, that's the fourth time I saw it today."

He stopped short. "Esther, you need to tell me those things."

"I need to tell you every time I count cars? I do it kind of a lot, along with steps and sidewalk cracks." She glanced behind them. "One thousand four hundred thirty three since Monday."

"No, the car. Did you see who drove?"

"Male, wearing a hat and sunglasses."

"Did you get the plate?"

"Maryland, DTV7205."

He blinked at her. "Why am I here again?"

"You have the gun. Guns." She touched his biceps and he laughed.

"Right. Let's get back and deliver our gift." He took her arm, wary this time, on the lookout for anyone who might be following.

CHAPTER 7

The party was a success, both for the parents-to-be and Esther, who sat serenely on the periphery and didn't ask one question about nursing or mention all that could go wrong with the birth or blurt infant mortality statistics for developed nations. (She did that once, but only to Leo.) In fact she sat tucked beside him, as friendly and relaxed as he'd ever seen her, unlike him who had now added a new worry. Had someone been following them today? And, if so, was that the first time?

He dithered throughout the party, distracted. When it was over, he told Esther to wait for him and reluctantly made his way to Ridge's office. As galling as it was that the man who had once been his rival was now his boss, it was even more humbling to have to ask for his counsel.

"Come in," Ridge said. He glanced up when Leo made his entrance, not quick enough to hide his surprise. "Leo, can I help you with something?"

Leo sat, letting his gaze travel around the cozy, well-appointed office. If he'd kept his nose clean, been less of a loose cannon, less cocky, less of a screwup, he might be the one in the office. Not that Cameron Ridge would ever wind up in Leo's position. Guys like him didn't sink that low. It was physically impossible for them to tumble from atop their white stallions.

"Esther and I went out today. I saw the same sedan twice. Esther saw it four times." He wasn't embarrassed to admit Esther saw the car more because she had also bested Ridge in her observations. With Esther, being observant wasn't a competition; she blew everyone else out of the water.

"Huh." Ridge steepled his fingers together and leaned back. "Anything else unusual to report?"

Leo smiled. "I'm assigned to Esther. My definition of the word unusual has become something else entirely."

Ridge laughed. "Yes, she's not what any of us expected."

Leo's smile morphed to a frown.

"We thought she'd be cocky," Ridge hastened to explain. "I mean, she was basically handpicked by the highest ranking military intelligence branch in the world, placed here with kid gloves, assigned her own handler. And yet she seems either unaware or unaffected by how unusual that is. And she's so..."

"Wholesome?" Leo supplied.

"Fresh off the farm," Ridge agreed. "I'm glad to see you two getting along so well. I had my doubts, actually. I thought you'd do a runner by now, if I'm being honest. This seems outside your comfort zone."

"It is, but..." he paused, not certain how to say it and not certain he wanted to. "Esther is...soothing."

"Sometimes we get so caught up in our world of life and death and secrets, it's shocking to meet someone from real life. Makes you remember your priorities. That was what happened with me and Maggie," Ridge explained. "Like my first breath after being underwater."

Leo remained silent, uncertain of how to respond. They were old school military, not exactly known for discussing the warm fuzzies.

"Yes, marriage has changed me," Ridge added, reading Leo's mind.

"Uh, good for you, I guess," Leo said. He swiped his hand over the back of his neck.

"As for being followed, I'll put Ethan on it, see if he can catch a tail.

Esther's been working on some high-level, high-priority stuff lately. If someone has found out about that…"

"It could only have come from this office," Leo inserted.

Ridge scowled, staring hard at his desk. "Not necessarily. Her hire made the paper. The contest was national news. It wouldn't take much for a high-level hacker to track her here. It might have to do with her newfound notoriety and nothing to do with our caseload."

"Sounds like wishful thinking to me," Leo said.

Ridge's lips tightened, but his voice was even when he replied, "Maybe so. We have a tightknit crew here. I'd hate to think we have a mole. But I also keep an open mind because we both know letting the job become personal is what trips us up."

"Is that a warning?" Leo asked.

"Not at all. Keep me informed. If I find anything, I'll do the same," Ridge said.

Leo took it as the dismissal it was. He stood and was almost at the door before Ridge spoke again.

"Leo."

Leo paused and turned back.

"I read the transcripts of what went down with your team. I had them sent over when I knew you'd be working here. You did nothing wrong. There is nothing you could have done differently, nothing to save those men. It's one of the risks of what we do."

"It's never happened to you," Leo said.

"No, but there have been close calls," Ridge said.

Leo gave him a heads up nod and let himself out. Ridge probably meant well, but until it happened, he couldn't know how it felt. *Survivor's guilt.* In this instance, knowing the correct word for it did nothing to alleviate the feelings burning inside him. Nothing he did ever seemed to ease the gnawing shame that he was the one who came home when others didn't.

Esther stood waiting in their cubicle, fingers twirling her braid. "I want you to navigate our way home," he said.

"Sure," she agreed.

"I didn't expect such easy agreement," he admitted. She never paid attention to their surroundings, never had the vaguest idea where they were when he asked her.

She shrugged one shoulder, giving him a half smile that looked different from the others, secretive, perhaps.

Once they were in the car, she told him which way to turn out of the parking lot. She called each turn before he reached it, taking them to her apartment with ease.

He double parked in the street and faced her. "I am thoroughly impressed."

"I memorized the map," she confessed.

"Have you been having late night study sessions?" he asked, smiling. She was an early-to-bed, early-to-rise person, a fact he'd discerned during their first week together.

"No, while you were talking to Ridge." She reached for the handle.

"Hold up. You memorized how to get home in the short time I talked to Ridge?"

"No, I memorized all the streets in DC."

He quizzed her, asking her to name the street four blocks away. When she answered correctly, he asked her to name all the streets surrounding their office. "Of course I only did metro DC," she added regretfully. "If we venture farther, I'm still lost."

"Esther." He picked up her braid and tickled the end of her nose, causing her to grimace. Light touches drove her crazy. He had no idea he knew that information until that moment.

She shuddered and rubbed her nose, chasing the feeling of stray hairs away. "What?"

"Nothing. I'm going to walk you up today."

"Okay," she said, not questioning him on it. She had never questioned him on anything. He could tell her they were going to dance the hula on a picnic table in the park, and she would reach for a lei and say, "okay."

"If it's so easy for you to navigate by memorization, why didn't you do it before?" he asked as they hoofed it up four flights of stairs in her building. He was *not* puffing or winded. He'd eaten more than usual today, that was all.

"Why would I do that when I have you?" she asked.

"Then why did you do it today?" he asked. He took her key and opened the door, pausing to make certain there were no sounds within. After possibly being followed today, he wasn't taking any chances.

"Because you want to get rid of me," she said. Her tone was the same frank one she always used, but his heart stuttered.

"Esther, I don't want to get rid of you," he said.

"Of course you do." She faced him, clasping her hands behind her back. "You want to move on to an assignment with more prestige and action. You don't want to be saddled with someone like me."

"What do you mean, someone like you?" he asked, annoyed. He had no idea why he was annoyed, he just was.

"Leo, come on."

"Come on what, Esther? What are you trying to say?"

"Eleutheromania."

"Use normal words," he said.

"These are my normal words," she replied.

"Fine. Good night, I'll see you in the morning." He turned and walked out of her apartment, closing the door sharply behind him. He hoofed it down all the flights of stairs and slid behind the wheel before he'd let himself reach for his phone and look up the word.

Eleutheromania: An intense and irresistible desire for freedom.

He tossed the phone onto the seat, frustrated with Esther, frustrated with himself, frustrated with everything. Why was he frustrated, though? Everything was true. He did want to get away from this assignment. He did want to get away from *her*. He could feel himself teetering over the edge, blurring the lines between the job and friendship. He couldn't go down that road again; he *wouldn't*. The guys on his team, they'd been his brothers, the closest people in the world to him. And now they were gone. And they had been trained soldiers and agents, like him. How much worse would it feel to lose someone so helpless, so soft and vulnerable and under his care?

He shuddered and turned up the air, feeling suddenly nauseated. The sooner he got Esther up to speed so he could move on, the better.

On the other hand, he didn't want to hurt her feelings, to make her think she was some kind of dread assignment. He wanted her to see the truth of the situation with no hurt feelings.

That's what she already did, he reminded himself. There had been no hurt or regret in Esther's tone. In fact she'd sounded chipper when she talked about moving on from their arrangement.

He wouldn't allow himself to think that was the source of his annoyance. He was supposed to be the one who wanted to move on, not her. She was the one with an inappropriate crush. Or was she? What made him believe she had feelings for him outside the realm of their working relationship? She'd certainly never acted on them, never hinted as much, never flirted with him, mooned over him, stared at him, fawned over him. On the contrary, she acted like any professional work mate should act, and wasn't that a kick in the teeth?

"You are some kind of messed up dude, Leo," he whispered to himself. The sooner he finished this assignment and moved on, the better everyone would be. *Eleutheromania,* indeed. Bring it, Leo was ready for freedom.

CHAPTER 8

As expected, the next morning Esther acted as if nothing was amiss. In her mind it probably wasn't. She wasn't one to dwell on things, wasn't a grudge holder, tended instead to focus only on what was currently right in front of her. Leo had started to depend on her unwavering steadiness, but he also knew how easy it would be to take advantage of it.

She slipped into the car and handed him his breakfast and coffee. "Thank you. I'm sorry about yesterday."

"What about yesterday?" she asked.

"We argued."

"We did?"

"Yes." He took a bite of breakfast, resisting the urge to close his eyes and make "yummy" noises. He wasn't certain if it was that good or if he was that starved for homemade food. Maybe both.

"Was I rude?" she asked.

"Horribly."

"Oh, I'm sorry," she said, sounding contrite.

He squeezed her knee. "Esther, I'm lying. You weren't rude. I became angry, snapped at you, and stormed away."

"Huh."

"You really didn't notice?" he asked.

She shook her head. "I must have done something to make you angry. No one gets angry for no reason."

"I do, actually. Last night, for example." He tapped his temple. "Lots going on in here, kid."

She rested her hand on his forearm. "That's not healthy, Leo. I worry about you. What's going to become of you when this is finished?"

"I'll go back to being hungry and miserable." He tried to be flippant and failed horribly. He had no idea until he said it that the misery had been absent the last few weeks. Whether it was due to Esther's steady presence or having a task that required his full focus, he didn't know. For the first time in years, he was fully engaged in his job, in his life. He had missed that feeling of engagement. For so long he'd been ghosting through life, detached, not depressed enough to end it but secretly wishing for it to be over. Was that why he drank so much? Why he rarely ate? Was that his passive way of trying to hasten his end?

Esther surprised him by hugging him and resting her head on his shoulder. "Leo." He hugged her in return and she shifted, nestling again. He liked that. It was a sort of gift, he thought, an abandonment of herself into his care. He kissed the top of her head and rested his head on it.

"Let's take the Metro today. We need to get you acclimated."

"Okay," she agreed.

"Stop being so agreeable," he warned.

"Okay."

"Give me a word before I decide to punish you for your insolence," he commanded.

"Consanguinity. It means close relationship or connection," she said.

"I already knew that."

She pulled away to peer up at him, smiling. "Did you?"

"No, Esther."

"Big fat sarcasm, my old nemesis," she said.

He brushed his thumb on her cheek. "You ready to Metro?"

"Yes," she said, but she didn't look ready. She looked reluctant and maybe a little afraid. Leo told himself they were doing this for her good, so she would be ready to do it without him when the time came. But as they teemed into the station along with the other swarming mass of humanity, he had to resist the urge to lead her back out again. So many people, so busy, so intent. And there was Esther, small, helpless, lost. She looked like a tourist. Worse than a tourist, she looked like someone new to the country, someone for whom English was a second language, someone too easy to take advantage of, misdirect, kidnap, wound.

He made her buy the ticket, standing watch behind her like Papa Grizzly. He made her insert it, waited until she went through the turnstile, and made his way inside. And that was when his skin started to prickle.

So many years in the military and intelligence had given him a sixth sense, a keen awareness of danger. Casually, he let his gaze drift around them as his hand reached out and clasped Esther's. If they had to run, he wanted to be prepared. Esther sensed nothing amiss, not in their surroundings, nor in the intimate joining of their hands. She remained staring down the track, watching for the train. Meanwhile Leo saw nothing out of place. No one watched them or hovered nearby. No one had anything that could be a weapon. But he refused to take the reassurance. Something was off, even if he couldn't see it.

Before he could decide to turn and walk out of the station, the train arrived. Esther tugged his hand, leading him forward. At this point it would be worse to go off on their own, opposite from everyone else. Herd mentality worked in their favor. Few people were willing to commit a crime in front of a crowd of witnesses.

They shuffled onto the train. Leo grabbed a strap and put his arm around Esther, pulling her snugly against him. It was a necessary gesture in the cramped space, but he did it so he could whisper in her ear.

"Do you see anyone on this train you recognize? Be subtle as you scan. Do it slowly and try not to draw attention to the gesture."

She turned and leaned on him, her back to his front. To anyone observing it would resemble a romantic posture, especially when he slipped his arm around her waist. But she was merely trying to get a better vantage point.

After a slow perusal of their fellow passengers, she turned, stood on her toes, and whispered in his ear. "Five people."

His hand tightened on her waist. Five? Were they being herded by an entire group? "Which five?" he croaked.

"The old lady three paces away works at the grocery store on my block. The man with blond curly hair works at the library I frequent. The man with red hair lives in the building next to mine, and the woman with natural hair works in the building next to ours."

"Who is the fifth person you recognize?" he asked.

"You."

It was such an Esther thing to say that he sputtered a laugh. "I wasn't supposed to be included on the list."

"You didn't specify," she said. Somehow through all the hard jostling of the train, they had shifted slightly. His hands were on her hips, her arms resting on his shoulders, her lips brushing his ear when she spoke.

"Have any of them ever followed you before, ever shown up somewhere unusual?" he asked.

She shook her head and rested it on his chest, nestling. He wrapped his arms around her and kissed the top of her head. If they were supposed to look like a couple in this moment, he might as well sell it.

When Leo was young and full of himself, he was never uncertain. He barreled toward every decision with the certainty only youth can bring. But now, after the school of hard knocks, he found himself in doubt. Why were they taking the Metro when it was riddled with danger? Eventually Esther would have to navigate the route herself; he wanted her well-trained for that moment. But was it crazy to train her when she was possibly being followed? Or was she being followed? Was he seeing phantoms because he was stressed about having her in his care? Suddenly he missed the cockiness of his youth. Uncertainty wasn't an emotion he would ever warm to. Then again, just because he'd been certain of an action back then didn't mean it was correct. He had gotten himself and his teammates in trouble more than once because he failed to listen, to take heed. Perhaps what he needed to work on in the future was finding a balance, learning to pause and check his gut before he acted.

What did his gut tell him right now? If someone was following them, the threat was low. At this point, teaching Esther to take over the reins of her own care outweighed a menace, real or imaginary. If someone revealed himself to be a danger, then Leo would neutralize. Until then, Esther needed to learn how to function in everyday life.

"Tell me when it's our stop," Leo whispered, his mouth conveniently close to her ear.

She straightened and stared hard at the map on the wall of the train. "We're next, I think, right?"

"I don't know. Are we?"

She gave him an annoyed little shove and stepped closer to the map, squinting. Leo watched other people watch her. An old woman smiled benevolently. Esther had the sort of wholesomeness that appealed to the older set, like she should be on a poster for Swiss tourism, her hair in braids, her hands busy milking a cow. One of the young men, the one who worked at the library she frequented, watched her with a different kind of interest, a kindling attraction. He took a step forward, as if he was going to approach. Leo shifted, unconsciously flexing, and the boy stepped back and looked away, blushing.

Was that all this was? Was Esther being pursued by a whelp who wanted to ask her out? Now Leo eyed Esther critically. Would she be interested in the boy? Had she ever been on a date? Was she as naïve about men as she was about everything else in life? Sometimes he felt like the day she arrived in DC was the day she first hatched into being. She had knowledge, too much knowledge. She could spout facts about everything. But she had zero street or common sense and a vague sort of detachment toward her emotions. And yet she had them. She was funny, kind, caring, sweet.

The robotic voice of the Metro announced the upcoming stop. Esther turned to Leo and held out her hand. "This is us, for certain."

Leo put his hand in hers and gave it a squeeze. "This is us, I agree."

CHAPTER 9

"Should we go?"

Esther glanced up as if shocked to realize Leo was in the room, even though he'd never left. She became fully immersed in her work, to the exclusion of everything else, including him.

"Out with everyone," he added.

Her perplexed frown deepened. "Is it a fire drill?"

"Everyone is going out after work. For food. They invited us."

"They did? When did they do that?"

"When Maggie was here," he said.

"Maggie was here?" she asked. She pushed away from the table and flexed her fingers. She had been using them to help her search the hundred faces before her, combing for hidden members of a familial crime syndicate. Leo usually insisted she take more breaks, but it was raining and dreary outside and he was tired, too tired to leave the quiet harmony of their little room. Now Esther was emerging from her work fog like Sleeping Beauty after her hundred year nap. He could see her eyes straying there again, back to the table, back to her work. He pushed it away.

"Let me recap. Everyone from work is going out tonight and we're invited. Do you want to go?"

"It seems like we probably should, right?" Esther said.

"It seems like we probably should, but if you don't want to, we don't have to." She sounded reticent.

"I do, it's just..."

"What?"

"Sometimes it feels like it's us and them. Not in a menacing way, but in a comfortable way. I like that we have our own bubble."

Leo did too, if he were being honest. He didn't particularly care to go out for forced bonding time with the crew, especially when his job was temporary. But that was why they needed to go. What would happen to Esther after he left? That question was foremost on his mind lately. She would sit in this cubicle and work until she starved to death, with no one to prompt her to eat, to get up and walk, to stretch, to take a break. And she certainly wouldn't bond with her coworkers who still tiptoed around her like she was a nuclear bomb that might accidentally go off if they bumped her too hard. They weren't mean to her, Leo would give them that. Some might even say they were kind. But it was clear they didn't understand her, didn't see the sweet softness under her blunt exterior. Thanks to what Babs had told him about Blue's fiancée, Jane, Leo thought they wanted to like Esther, were giving her extra allowances in case she was merely anxious. But how long would those allowances last? After Leo's part in this was finished, Esther would be on her own. She wouldn't seek friendships with her coworkers. Maybe she wouldn't notice the lack of social interaction, but what if she did? What if, without him, she felt isolated and alone? It was a painful thought, breaking up their duo, only for her to become a lone wolf.

"We're going to go, and we're not going to talk to each other. We have to talk to other people," Leo said.

She sighed and massaged her fingers. "The closer it gets to your departure, the bossier you become. By the end, you're going to club me over the head and drag me places."

"Only for your own good," Leo said, grinning when she poked him. Despite her words, she wasn't irritated with him. She was nearly impossible to goad. The only thing that seemed to set her off was an unexpected light touch. Leo didn't do it, but occasionally someone brushed against her and she would shudder and rub the spot. When he questioned her on it once, she told him it felt like millions of tiny ants had been set loose under her skin.

They walked to the restaurant, only a few blocks from work. Leo once again had the prickling sensation alerting him to danger, but there was no visible reason for it. In his newfound zeal to be a team player, he had told Ridge and Ethan his suspicious feeling on the Metro a few days ago. Ridge said he appreciated the heads up. Ethan said he'd been scouting Esther's building and dogging her on her days off, but he hadn't observed anything suspicious. Secretly Leo wondered if they thought he was crazy or, worse, too emotionally vested in Esther to be objective. Was he? Was he seeing monsters everywhere because she was so innocent and unprotected? He shoved the thought away and hoped it never came back. He was listening to his gut. His gut told him something was off, even if he couldn't put his finger on it.

The restaurant was packed with the after-work crowd. It was a dark place, basically a hole in the wall, with a walk up bar, several wooden tables, and a few ratty booths. Their group sat at the back, of course, near an exit, able to see everyone who entered. Leo did his usual scan of the place, looking for anyone or anything who didn't belong. Esther tumbled blindly toward their crew, determination etched in her face. He could practically hear her thoughts. *Leo says I need to be social, so that's what I'm going to do.* But she couldn't, at least not at first, because Leo hailed her back. He latched onto her arm and leaned in to speak low in her ear.

"Note the exits. Decide which one you'll take in an emergency. Look around. See if there's anyone you recognize, see if you've been followed." She stopped short and started to scan. He rolled his eyes. "Covertly. Think like a spy. For goodness sake, woman, you're turning my hair several shades of gray."

Now her gaze fastened on his hair, literal, as usual. "Huh, a little," she agreed and gave him an understated smile when he raised his hand self-consciously to his head. "I thought we weren't supposed to talk to each other."

"I'm making an exception in order to bestow wisdom. You should be writing it down; it's good stuff, Quantico level," he said. Maybe she should go to Quantico. He would talk to Ridge about it. Esther was aces at all things academic. If a teacher or book told her to do something, she would soak it in like sponge.

"Sarcasm," she noted with a little nod.

"Not sarcasm. Raw truth. Everything I say is worthy of being bronzed or, at the very least, branded into your memory," he declared.

"Everything you say is branded into my memory, but then again everything anybody says is, so..." she gave a helpless little shrug and scooted into the booth beside a knockout blond Leo didn't recognize. Before he could gear himself up to hit on her, Maggie introduced her.

"Leo and Esther, this is my little sister, Amelia."

"And my wife," Ethan added swiftly. He tossed Leo a look. *At ease, Marine. She's taken.*

Leo gave him a little smile and nod. *Ah, got it. Kudos on that.*

Ethan gave him a nod of acknowledgment in return and that was that.

Amelia, meanwhile, hadn't seemed to notice Leo at all, so taken was she with Esther. "Oh, my goodness, look at your hair. It's gorgeous." Uninvited, she picked up Esther's braid and inspected it, measuring it against the width of her hand. "I mean, seriously. The color, the texture, the length. You know how much you could sell this for? I bet when it's wet it hangs down to your hips."

"So, Amelia's a stylist," Ethan inserted.

"Not a black market scalper, as it currently appears." This was said by a newcomer, a tall man with dark hair, his hand firmly clasped onto Babs.

"You must be the brother," Leo said. "I'm Leo, this is Esther."

"Darren," he replied. "Babs has told me a lot of great things."

Leo glanced at Babs, assessing her reaction to the statement. She didn't flush or seem embarrassed, meaning the things she'd passed along must actually have been positive. Not, *The new people at work are total freaks who keep to themselves all the time,* like he imagined.

"Where are Jane and Blue?" Amelia asked.

"Jane had a thing at the museum," Maggie said.

"Boo," Amelia pouted. "Ridge needs to hire Jane so she'll stop having stuff outside of us."

"You be the one to suggest it," Ethan said.

Smiling, Amelia turned her attention on Esther again. "You should come by the salon sometime. I would love to do something with this." She picked up Esther's thick braid again. "And with a little makeup to highlight your amazing bone structure, you'd be unstoppable."

"Careful, Mel, you're making Leo scowl. It took us until last week to get him to stop scowling in the first place," Ethan cautioned.

"My family isn't really into makeup and hairstyles," Esther confessed. She didn't sound reluctant; she sounded excited. Leo's scowl deepened.

"I think Esther's fine as she is," he said.

Amelia and Esther turned to bestow a smile on him. "Newsflash, Leo: women don't dress for men," Amelia said. "Don't be one of those guys."

"One of what guys?" he asked, slightly defensive. She clearly wasn't as sweet natured as her sister.

"One of those guys who is afraid of change, who thinks long hair is everything, who possessively doesn't want another man looking at what he believes is his," Amelia expounded.

"Esther isn't mine," he explained, his patience wearing thin. "But she is innocent and wholesome. I don't think making her into a femme fatale would be doing anyone any favors."

Amelia rolled her eyes, annoyed, but Esther beamed at him. "You said femme fatale and used it correctly. I'm so proud."

"Femme fatale. Please," Amelia scoffed.

"Esther's mother is a midwife," Maggie, ever the peacemaker, interjected. She was solo, for the moment. Ridge was the kind of boss who believed in going down with the ship. He was routinely the last left standing at the end of the day.

"Really?" Amelia asked, with renewed interest. "That's fascinating. I've considered becoming a doula, as a side gig." Her head snapped toward her brother. "Not a word from you about quackery."

Darren made a zipping motion across his lips. Babs patted his leg approvingly.

"Babe, you work sixty hours a week. Exactly where would this free time come from?" Ethan asked.

"Not now, but maybe someday in the future. I can't keep up these crazy hours after we have kids."

Maggie perked up. "Kids? You're talking kids now?"

"This is the first I've heard of it," Ethan said.

"We're not talking kids, yet. But I'm a planner, always thinking ahead," Amelia said, tapping her temple. "What about you, Esther. Are you dating anyone? Attached?"

"No, I was, sort of, before I left home. But it didn't work out," Esther said.

"Leo's scowling again," Ethan noted.

Leo smoothed his expression. He had pictured Esther as being a solitary, untouched figure, and now he found out she had a boyfriend? His protectiveness was riled once again. Was that why she left? Had the guy mistreated her? *This must be how big brothers feel all the time,* he mused. He didn't like it; it was exhausting. He opened his mouth to respond to Ethan's teasing, not realizing their world was about to explode into utter chaos and mayhem.

He felt the change before he saw it, a crackling awareness of danger. Ethan felt it, too. Leo saw him stiffen, and then he saw something else: a red dot in the center of Esther's forehead.

Leo had seen a lot of action in his lifetime, and it always went down the same way, as if everything was on fast forward and pause at the same time. Multiple things happened at once, but Leo saw each with clarity. "Get down," he yelled, shoving Esther under the table. The seat beside him exploded in a shower of wooden shrapnel. Someone screamed—Amelia, maybe?—Ethan flipped the table, using it as a shield and barrier, his gun bared. Around them people were screaming, running, scurrying, diving.

In the doorway at the back of the restaurant stood the gunman, covered head to toe in gear—a helmet, vest. He was heavily armored, too much for Leo to get a decent shot. He hoped Ethan was a better marksman than he was.

"Ethan, your gun," Maggie demanded coolly, and Ethan handed it over without protest. Before Leo could register the shocking exchange, the gunman fired off another shot, his last. A second later, he fell backwards, a neat hole in the center of his forehead.

For a second, nobody from their group moved. Leo and Ethan were still on alert. Had the guy acted alone? Would someone else come through the door, gun drawn?

"Everyone okay?" Ethan asked. His free hand rubbed a soothing little circle on Amelia's back. She lay beside him on the floor, shoulders quivering with repressed tears.

"We're okay," Darren said shakily. He sat up and put a hand down for Babs, running his hands up and down her arms, either checking for injuries or bestowing warmth. Of everyone they had been in the most danger, on the fringe of the group, closest to the gunman. He could easily have taken them out, but he hadn't been aiming for them.

Ridge entered then, dismayed, gun at his side. He looked at the dead man on the ground and the gun still clutched in his wife's hand, knowing immediately what happened. He sat beside her, peeled the gun out of her clenched fingers, and handed it to Ethan. "Hon," he said, questioningly. His arm slid around her shoulders, while his free hand rested on her extended bump.

She gave him a nod.

Leo released the breath he didn't know he'd been holding and finally faced Esther. He had been keeping her in his peripheral, so he knew she was safe, at least physically. But most of them had been privy to gunfire before. For Esther, this was a whole new, ugly world. Sure enough, when he looked at her, her eyes were luminous with shock.

"Es," he tried to say, but the words wouldn't form.

"Leo, you're shot," she whispered. She reached out to press her hand to his shoulder, drenched with blood. Leo looked down at the bloody mess. A bit of shock faded away, to be replaced with a roar of pain, loud enough to fill his brain. Esther moved closer, cradling him, his blood marring the perfection of her cardigan.

"Esther," he tried again, and everything faded to a hazy shade of gray.

CHAPTER 10

"A clean shot, through and through. No bone, no arteries."

Ethan's calm assessment broke through the haze. Leo wasn't certain if he was trying to reassure Esther or merely stating a fact.

"There's a lot of blood," Esther said. Her voice sounded small, afraid, but not shaky. She wasn't crying, wasn't falling apart. In the distance, sirens blared, growing ever closer. Leo needed to wake up, but the pull of blissful unconsciousness was so strong. His shoulder burned like someone had stuffed a live coal in there. Going back to sleep would provide him blessed reprieve. But, no, he had something important to stay awake for. What, though?

"You're going to be okay, Leo," Esther whispered sweetly in his ear. Ah, right. Her. He forced his eyes open and tried to sit up.

Ethan's hand was a weight on his shoulder, holding him down, holding him together. "Easy there, Marine. You have a bit of a hole in your shoulder. Stay still."

"Ridge," Leo rasped. His boss's face popped into view above him, looking serious and concerned. "Need to talk to you. Important."

"I have to stay and deal with the police, specifically to explain how my very pregnant wife is an expert marksman. I'll catch up with you at the hospital."

"Esther," Leo rasped, but he was still talking to Ridge. Esther needed to be taken care of; Esther was being hunted.

"We'll take care of Esther," Ridge promised.

"I'm going with Leo," Esther said, enough steel in her tone to make him smile. Not many people had the courage to stand up to Cameron Ridge.

Leo faded before he could hear the resolution to the conversation, but it must have ended in Esther's favor because when the ambulance arrived and loaded him on the cart, she was beside him, quiet and intense in the background, her delicate features shrouded with worry. "I'm going to be fine." He tried to say it in an assuring tone, but it lost something when it rasped weakly from dry lips.

"Sangfroid," she whispered.

He smiled, wincing when his dry bottom lip cracked. "What's that one?"

Esther reached into her bag, pulled out lip balm, and smeared it on his suffering lips. Knowing what a germaphobe she was, it was a big concession. "Coolness of mind, calmness."

"The marines trained me well. You, though, you're a natural, apparently."

She shook her head hard. He wondered if she was about to crack, to break down in tears. The medics stepped between them, taking Leo's vitals, starting an IV, asking probing questions about his health and allergies. Leo answered with clipped, one word answers, both because he was in pain and because he was worried. With him out of the game, what was to stop someone from getting to Esther? She was so vulnerable, so exposed.

He felt another flicker of amusement when they arrived at the hospital and the medics tried to steer Esther to the lobby.

"No, I'm going with Leo." Her tone was quiet, resolute. Leo guessed they dealt with so many hysterical people her cool reserve baffled and disturbed them. Whatever the reason, she once again prevailed, accompanying him to his cubicle where they were left alone for the first time since the shooting occurred.

"Are you doing okay?" he whispered, fervent in case they were interrupted again.

"Leo, you're the one who is shot."

"Newsflash, kid, not my first time. It is your first time dealing with this stuff, though."

"I'm not as delicate as you think I am," she told him.

"I have never once thought you were delicate," he said. Naïve and wholly unaware of the world around her, yes. Delicate and weak, no.

"What can I get you?" she asked. "Our meal was interrupted. You must be starved."

"I'm fine, Esther. Just…don't leave my side, okay? I need you beside me at all times."

"I'm always beside you, Leo. We're practically a host and fungi by now," she said. "Shark and lamprey, hippo and bird."

"Holmes and Watson," he inserted, smiling in amusement when she wrinkled her nose. For some reason she didn't enjoy the comparison. He wasn't certain if comparing her to Sherlock felt too elevated or comparing him to Watson felt too demeaning. Maybe both things. In any case, she was often swift to point out that, in their duo, he was the one who called the shots.

A nurse came in to redo everything that had already been done in the ambulance—vitals, history, allergies. She added more pain reliever to his IV, checked his wound, and told him the doctor would be in shortly.

An hour later, the doctor arrived and did a painful exam, probing the wound. Leo tried not to, but he couldn't stop a few winces and gasps from escaping.

"Good news and more good news," the doctor said, pushing the bright light away from Leo's shoulder. "It went straight through in a clean shot, no fragments, no bone splinters, no arteries. You're going to need physical and possibly occupational therapy and lots of it. And it's going to hurt, but you'll be fine. I'm so confident you don't need surgery we're going to skip x-rays. I do, however, intend to keep you overnight. You've lost a lot of blood, and infection is always a possibility. We have some antibiotics and pain reliever flowing in your IV. I'm going to put in my orders, and we'll have you in a room in no time."

"No time," turned out to be three hours later. Ridge waited in his room.

"You're starting to give off Colonel vibes," Leo said. Their boss was well known for his near prescient omnipresence. He also had a habit of showing up in the most unlikely places in a timely manner.

Ridge smiled. "I'll take that as a compliment. How are you doing, Leo?"

"Fine," Leo said. From a marine to a sailor, there was no other possible answer to that question. "How's Maggie?"

"She'll be okay. We've always talked about the possibility that she'd have to take a kill shot, but it all seemed theoretical, and certainly not something we expected in late pregnancy. But it was clear there was no other option."

"There was no other option," Leo said. "She saved lives," his gaze darted to Esther, "I hope she knows."

"She does, at least in her head. The heart's another matter, but I'm hoping the baby's arrival will help soothe things. The first kill is always the hardest, as you know."

Leo gave a heads up nod in agreement.

"You said there was something you needed to tell me," Ridge prompted.

Leo's gaze darted to Esther again. She was curled in a chair, a too-thin blanket draped over her tiny frame. "They were coming for her," he blurted. Esther might look fragile, but what he said earlier was true —she wasn't a fading flower. And she had the right to know the stark truth of the situation.

"Whoever the guy was wasn't very bright because he left the red dot sight on. If I hadn't seen it…" he didn't finish, but he didn't have to. Esther might not be alive. In fact, they all might be dead. Just because he and Ethan had sensed danger at the same moment didn't mean they would have been able to properly identify it. Lucky for them it identified itself in time to prevent tragedy. "Any idea who he was?"

"A merc. Blue's working on who hired him."

A trained soldier for hire wouldn't come cheap. Not many people had that kind of bankroll. "He knew where we were. He knew where we'd be sitting," Leo said.

"Yes," Ridge agreed, not breaking eye contact. The foreknowledge smacked of a mole. "I spoke to The Colonel. We've arranged a safe house for when you're out of here, which should be tomorrow, if the rumors are true. Esther is staying here for the night, I presume."

"You presume correctly," Esther said.

"Good. I'll post a guard at the door. He reached into his pocket and deposited a set of keys on the table between them, along with a folded piece of paper. "A car and the address of the house. Check back in three days, safe channels."

Leo gave him the heads up nod again.

Ridge turned toward the door and paused, his hand on the frame. "Take care of yourselves and each other. And I guess it goes without saying not to trust anyone." He didn't wait for a reply before easing out the door, leaving silence in his wake.

Leo stared at the door a long time after he left, thinking. When he said the last about not trusting anyone, why did it sound like he included himself?

"Do you want me to get you some food?" Esther's gentle voice invaded his dark thoughts. He turned to survey her. She was still curled in the chair, looking more exhausted than he'd ever seen her. But of course her first thought was for him.

"No, you're not allowed to leave my side, remember?" he said.

"They have this thing called delivery," she said.

"Was that sarcasm?" he asked, aghast.

"Was it?" she asked, equally aghast. "It wasn't supposed to be. It was factual information. I could have something delivered for you."

Between the pain reliever and pain, he felt nauseated more than anything else. "I'm fine, but you must be starved."

"I don't eat as much as you," she said. She tried to smile, but it looked a little wobbly.

"C'mere," he said.

She stood and came to the bed, hovering uncertainly. "I don't want to hurt you."

"It hurts more to have you far away," he said, patting the spot beside him with his good hand. Even that small motion hurt his injured shoulder. Shoulder injuries took forever to heal, would impede nearly every movement for weeks to come. It would be an aggravating inconvenience when Leo needed to be at his best. Esther lay down beside him. Leo slid his arm around her, and she nestled into him as usual, pressing her nose to the little spot beside his collarbone that seemed to be on reserve for her.

"You smell like blood," she noted, dispelling any notion that she enjoyed the comforting reassurance of his embrace as much as he enjoyed hers.

"Sorry," he said, a bit snappish.

"I wasn't complaining, merely stating fact. I spew facts when I feel self-conscious."

"You spew facts all the time."

"I'm self-conscious a lot," she said. "Are you sure I can't get you some food?"

"Why are you always trying to feed me, Esther?"

"It's the only way you'll let me take care of you," she said.

He blinked at that. "That's not true."

"Yes it is. You do everything for me. You tell me where to go, when to be there, what not to say. You've been trying your hardest to try and make me normal, to help me assimilate, to teach me how to navigate the city and the new job. And on top of all that you protect me. You…" she took a shuddery little breath, "you take bullets for me." She pressed her face to his armpit, nestling closer.

He smoothed his hand down her spine, wondering if she would cry. She shuddered a few times, but her eyes remained dry. "Esther," he said at last, "I hate to bust up this little heroic picture you're painting of me, but all those things you listed are in my job description."

"Doesn't mean I can't be thankful for them," she noted, her voice muffled against his chest.

His hand smoothed up and down her spine, soothing her with a firm touch. Esther went boneless, melting into him, stretching as she sighed.

"We need to figure out who's trying to kill you," he said.

"Okay," she replied sleepily, eyes closed.

"Esther, this is important," he warned. "Too important for sleep."

"I do my best thinking with my eyes closed."

"No, you don't. You're falling asleep," he accused.

"So sleepy, Leo. Next time someone shoots at us, let's make it be in the morning," she mumbled.

"Esther, wake up."

"Mm."

His finger skittered lightly on her forearm. She jumped away from him like she'd been branded, rubbing hard at the spot, scowling now. "What was that for?"

"To get you to wake up."

"I'm awake, and I don't know who shot you. Now what?"

"Now we plot our escape."

CHAPTER 11

The great thing about Esther was that she only argued when she truly felt she was right about something. That meant she generally only dug her heels in when it came to work, and since she was paid to be a human computer, Leo almost always deferred to her on work matters. But when it came to nearly everything else, she was willing to follow his lead, almost blindly. For instance, when he told her they were going to sneak out of a guarded hospital room and escape into the night, she sat up, straightened her clothes, and said, "What can I do to help?" Genius woman, in all the ways.

"That was easier than I thought it would be," she said now as Leo steered the agency's car out of the lot. "The guard let us walk right out."

"He wasn't guarding people from us, we were allowed to move around."

"Isn't he going to sound the alarm when we don't come back?" she asked.

"Probably, but we'll be long gone by then," Leo said.

"Gone where?"

When he didn't answer, she turned to survey him.

"I'm thinking," he supplied.

"Aren't we going to the safe house?" she asked.

"No."

"Why not?"

"We can't trust anything from the agency right now, not until I'm certain it hasn't been compromised."

"But we're in an agency car," she pointed out.

He turned to grin at her. "Esther, how do you feel about grand theft auto?"

"We're going to steal a car?" she squeaked.

"Of course not. I'm injured and, even without the shoulder wound, people find me suspicious. Too thuggish. You, on the other hand, you're sweet as Sunday pie."

"What's Sunday pie?" she asked.

"Pie so sweet it can walk right up and steal a car." He parked across from a gas station, watching. "There's always one person who leaves their car running while they go inside. We'll wait for that to happen and then you'll snatch it."

"But stealing is wrong," Esther said.

"Yes, it is. But this isn't a normal situation. We need to ditch this agency car, with all its bugs and tracking devices, and find a clean car. And then another one after that. And we'll need to buy a burner phone. First things first, that lady is getting ready to go inside. Go boost her car."

"But I can't take things that don't belong to me."

When he faced her, she looked so upset he had second thoughts. "Esther, being a spy is never black and white. Sometimes we do bad things for a good reason. Think of Maggie tonight. She killed a man, but she did it to protect us. Do you see what I'm saying?"

"Yes, but if I take that woman's car, she's going to suffer."

"We'll leave it somewhere easy to find in perfect condition, I promise. We're temporarily borrowing it, okay? She'll get it back." She bit her lip, still looking uncertain. He reached over and pressed his palm to her cheek. "I'm going to need you to trust me on this."

The uncertainty was still in her eyes, but she nodded, slipped from the car, got behind the wheel, and drove off, Leo following behind her.

A couple of blocks away, she pulled to the curb. Leo ditched the agency car and jogged up to stand beside the window. "Are you going to let me in?"

"I think I should be the one to drive," she said.

"You don't know how to drive; you don't have a license," he pointed out.

"I've read all the books, I know all the laws. I merely lack practice. And you're injured, medicated, exhausted." The steel was in her tone, the one that told him arguing would be pointless. Stuffing protests aside, he walked to the passenger side and slid inside. Truth be told, he was exhausted. He wanted nothing more than to let go and have someone else be in charge for a while. But Esther weighed a hundred pounds on a good day, had never driven before, had just stolen a car, had also been shot at, was wanted by someone still unknown, and was completely without guile. Leo was not off the clock, not by a longshot.

"Where to?" she asked.

"We'll have to get a motel room, I guess. Did you bring your usual wad of cash?" he asked.

She shook her head. "You told me not to, remember?"

He rubbed a spot between his brows. "Why do you always listen to me? How much do you have on you?"

"A thousand."

"Combined with what I have, that makes a thousand and ten dollars," he said. She sputtered a laugh, and he smiled, reached over, and squeezed her leg. "You're doing great, Esther, and this will all get figured out soon. Everything is going to be fine."

She darted him a little smile. "I trust you, Leo."

They were quiet a few minutes before she spoke again. "Leo."

"Mm." He couldn't, *wouldn't* fall asleep on her, but exhaustion dragged at his edges, trying hard to suck him under. He felt as if he were floating in some nether region, his body already succumbed, his mind still half alert.

"Where are we going?"

They were heading out of the city, a good thing. DC had too many cops and too many cameras. "We need somewhere anonymous, somewhere we can hide. It would be great if we could get off the grid for a while." He said the last ruefully. There was nowhere on the eastern seaboard off the grid anymore, except possibly parts of northern Maine. But that was much too far away. They needed to be within driving distance of DC in case he needed to call for ammo or backup. All he needed was a buffer, somewhere to lie low for a while and figure things out.

"Leo."

"Mm."

"I think I might know a place."

He perked up. "Really? Where?"

"Do you trust me?"

"Always."

"Good. Go to sleep. I'll wake you when we get there."

"I don't think I'll be able to sleep. You've never driven before. That would be crazy."

"There's no traffic," she said.

"Still…"

She reached over and squeezed his leg. "Leo, go to sleep."

It was the permission he needed to let go of the last threads of consciousness. A minute later, he was out.

He woke an hour later, startled by the realization he'd been unconscious. He jumped, his wound tugged painfully, and he closed his eyes again, fighting a wave of nausea.

"We should get some food in you," Esther said softly. She reached over and pressed her palm to his brow. It felt so good, so comforting that Leo closed his eyes again and leaned into her touch.

"We need a new car," he croaked.

"There's a town up ahead, the last one for a while. I'll drive through McDonalds for food, then we can steal a car."

Despite his misery, he snickered. "You've settled into a life of crime with a disturbing amount of ease."

"Maybe I was born to be a villain," she returned.

He opened his eyes a crack, watching her cherubic profile as she stared hard at the road. "If you're the devil, it's his best disguise yet."

She swung through McDonalds and ordered a meal for each of them. Leo should have been hungry, but his stomach revolted at the thought of food. He forced himself to eat anyway, knowing his body needed fuel. The soda was the only thing that held any appeal, and he gulped greedily. They used the bathroom, a difficult task for Leo with only one arm. No way he was asking for Esther's help with that part, however. He'd do it alone or die trying. She would likely die, if he asked her. He would bet everything he owned that she had never seen a man unclothed before. Then again she had said she had a boyfriend. What did he know about her, really? He had been careful to keep the line between work and personal life separate, never venturing too far over. He knew the essence of Esther—good, kind, crazy smart, hidden sense of humor. But the facts of her life were still a blur, mostly because he hadn't asked to know them.

They returned to the car. Esther had cleaned up all their trash and was currently removing any fuzz from the seats. "I want it to be really clean when the lady gets it back," she explained.

"The sooner we boost another car, the sooner she'll get this one back."

"Another gas station?" she guessed.

"Nah, it's too late at night. Not many people are stupid enough to leave their car running unattended at this hour."

"Where can we find someone stupid?" she asked.

"Let's head to a bar."

He drove down the road to the town's lone bar. It hadn't closed yet, was still going strong, in fact, if the blaring music streaming out was any indication. Leo parked and used his good arm to feel on top of the front tire a few times until he held up a key in triumph.

"Drunks lose their keys, so they often leave them on the tire for safekeeping. Why are people so predictable, Esther?"

"We don't all fit that mold," Esther said. She plucked the key from Leo's fingers and shooed him toward the passenger side. He was too sore and exhausted to argue. She adjusted the seat, nose wrinkled. "It smells bad in here."

"I'd venture to say this car has taken the brunt of too much beer a time or two," Leo mused. "We might be saving lives with this heist. Guy was probably going to drive drunk."

"That probably shouldn't make me feel better about stealing his car, but it does," Esther said, sounding happy and more than a little relieved. "Will the lady really get her car back soon? You don't think they'll impound it or anything do you?"

"Sweetheart, stop worrying about the lady. Her car is fine."

"I left her money for gas," she admitted. "In the console."

"How much?" Leo asked.

"A hundred dollars," she said, darting him a glance. "I don't actually know how much gas costs, never having gotten it before. Was that enough?"

"That was enough, Es." He stifled a yawn.

"Go to sleep, Leo. It's a long drive."

"I don't want to abandon you. What if you fall asleep?"

"I won't."

"How do you know?" he asked.

"Because I'll tell myself not to," she replied.

Said by anyone else, he would have scoffed, but Esther did seem to have perfect discipline over her body, much more than he did, apparently, if the way his eyes drifted shut was any indication. He wanted to tell her to wake him, if she needed a break. "If you need me…" he began, but the words faded as unconsciousness once again dragged him under. He wasn't certain if it was his imagination that fueled her reply or if it was real.

"I always need you, Leo," she said, her words ghostlike and gauzy, the last thing he remembered before sleep claimed him completely.

CHAPTER 12

The lulling clickety-clack of a railway roused Leo from his slumber. He was taken back in time to an assignment in Europe, one that included a ride on a train. If not for the fact that he got into a fistfight with a Russian snitch, it would have been a pleasant journey. "Where are we?" he croaked without opening his eyes. It was bright, past dawn. Already the sun hurt his head. His mouth tasted like he'd been using paste sticks as lollypops.

"New York," Esther said.

"Good. The city is anonymous."

"Leo, we're not in the city," Esther said. If he didn't know better, he might say her tone was wry. With effort, he pried his eyes open, looked out his window, and did a double take when a horse stared back at him. The clickety-clack hadn't been from a railroad, but rather the sound of horse hooves on roadway. Not much surprised Leo these days; he'd seen it all. But the sight of a horse four inches from his face was enough to leave him speechless. Esther laughed and the car turned left. Leo blinked, disbelieving. The town had the trappings of modernity—restaurants, stop lights, gas stations. But tied up at each store was a horse and buggy.

"What is this place?" he asked.

"Home," Esther replied, sounding weary and resigned, all at once.

"You're…you're Amish?" Leo asked, well and truly shocked.

"Leo, my last name is Stoltzfus."

He blinked at her. "So? I thought maybe your family was German."

"We are," she said, motioning around them. "But I'm not actually Amish. I'm Mennonite."

"What's the difference?" he asked.

"Electricity and buttons," she said in a way that let him know it was likely an old joke. "My parents were raised Amish and left."

"So, are they, what's the word, shunned?"

"No, they left during their rumspringa."

"You say that word like it should have meaning to me," he said.

"It's a time in an Amish child's life when they're given freedom to experiment with everything outside the religion. It's also the time when they're allowed to leave the faith, before they're baptized."

"Why doesn't everyone leave?" he asked. "It must be a hard life."

"It's…complicated. The strings of community are thick. Without it, you're left on your own."

"You said your parents weren't shunned," he reminded her.

"Shunned isn't the same as not being part of the community. For instance, when we have get togethers, my family isn't allowed to eat with everyone else."

"So they are shunned," he said.

"No," she said, shaking her head in frustration. "Shunning is hard core. Despite how the media makes it seem, it doesn't happen often, and it doesn't happen lightly. When you're shunned, it's as if you don't exist. No one is allowed to look at you or talk to you. You are ostracized, completely, until you repent. I still have relationship with my extended family, there are merely a few specific restrictions."

"Wait a minute, we can't go to your home. Whoever is tracking you has insider information. They'll follow us here," he said. His brain felt sluggish. Who was he kidding? His everything felt sluggish. Now that his meds had worn off, pain had made a vengeful return. It rippled through him, causing his teeth to chatter. He clamped them together and clenched the fist on his good hand.

"This isn't exactly my home. This is where my aunt and uncle live. It's off the grid, not connected to me in any way."

They wended their way through town, such as it was, and to an oversized white farmhouse. Several barns and buildings hovered unobtrusively in the background. The one thing that made the house stand out, at least to Leo, was the lack of wires. No electricity. No cable. No telephone. In the back, far from the house, was a tiny little building on blocks.

"Is that what I think it is?" he asked Esther.

"What do you think it is?" she replied.

"An outhouse."

"Then yes, that's what you think it is," she said. She parked the car. No one appeared to greet them, but Leo still had the sense they were being watched. It took effort to scrape himself from the car. His body had grown sore, stiff, and weak during the long ride. Esther came around to link her arm with his, offering assistance. She was too little to be of much physical service, but the gesture was comforting. Everything about Esther was comforting, he realized. She was turning into his lifesize security blanket. *More like an Amish quilt,* he thought before quickly shoving away his thoughts to focus on the task at hand.

They limped to the door and Esther knocked. It was answered by an Amish woman of indiscernible age. She might have been his age, his mother's age, Esther's age. With her hair pulled into a severe bun, no makeup, and ubiquitous Amish shirt and skirt, it was hard to carbon date her.

"Esther," she said, and that was the last word Leo understood for the next forty minutes. Esther spoke some gibberish, motioning occasionally to Leo. The woman spoke gibberish in return, looking more than a little shocked and concerned. Esther stood on her toes, peeled up his sleeve, and showed the woman his injury. She clucked her tongue, her concerned tone deepening to outright worry.

They were invited inside where the conversation continued. Leo had spent considerable time in Germany as a young marine. While there he picked up a handful of words. None of those sounded like these. Unable to understand a syllable of what was being said, he turned his attention instead to inspecting the house.

The kitchen was massive, the size of his entire apartment. The table was equally as large, solid oak, with ten matching chairs. To his right was a giant wood stove. The day was chilly and the stove was apparently in charge of heating the house. Leo had no idea what it was like upstairs in the bedrooms, but the kitchen was toasty warm, almost unbearably so. He rested his head in his hand, fighting against the pull of sleep. Esther put her hand on his good shoulder and rubbed a soothing little circle.

The woman, presumably the aunt, stood, her tongue clucking again. Esther stood and gathered Leo's hand in her smaller one.

"Come on, Leo." He wondered if they were heading upstairs, but no. They went through the kitchen and out the back door to a smaller house, tiny in comparison to the other. Unlike the warm and inviting kitchen they'd just left, the small house was closed up, slightly musty, dark, and cold. Esther and the aunt began opening curtains. They spoke a moment more, the aunt pointing to something, and then she was gone. Esther bent and began building a fire in the centrally located woodstove. This one wasn't as large as its cousin in the main house, but then it didn't have to be.

Leo watched her, mesmerized. He wasn't much of an outdoorsman, hadn't built a fire since his survival training. Esther did it as if it were routine. He wondered if it was, wondered how many times she'd done it in the past. Seemingly within moments she had it going and added a few small sticks of wood. Satisfied that it had caught and would take off, she began selecting which wood she would add next, tilting her head, sorting through the stack. Leo realized he was waiting for her to speak. A normal person would fill him in on everything he'd missed, but Esther wasn't a normal person.

"Esther, what was that? What happened? Where are we? What did you tell her about our situation?"

She faced him, tearing her attention off the piece of wood in her grasp with effort. "Hmm? Oh. That was my aunt Lydia. She and my mom are sisters. This was her husband's parents' house. We call it the *Dawdy haus*."

"Why?"

"Because that's what we call our grandparents, *Dawdy* and *Gross-mammi*. When they reach a certain age, the oldest son takes over the family homestead and the *Dawdy* moves into a smaller house, sort of like retirement. They get to stop working, to be cared for. His parents lived here until they died a couple of years ago. She's letting us stay here for a bit, for as long as we need."

"Just like that?" he asked. "Your Amish aunt is letting us stay in her in-law's house out of the blue, no questions asked?"

"Oh, well I told her you were a policeman and you've been injured, that we needed a quiet spot for you to recuperate."

"That makes sense for me, but what about you? Why does she think you're here?" he asked. He felt like there was something he was missing. Esther had already returned her attention to her wood selection and fire. She added the piece in her grasp and brushed her hands together before turning to face him again.

"Oh, I told her we're married."

CHAPTER 13

L eo stared at Esther, trying to read past the bland expression and flat tone, but she was still a blank.

"You lied to your Amish aunt? You told your family we're married?"

"Yes."

"Why?"

"She wouldn't have let me stay with you otherwise, and you said you needed me with you at all times."

"But you lied. To your Amish aunt." Was it a double sin to lie to an Amish person? It seemed like it should be.

"You said sometimes you have to find the gray area when you're a spy."

"You certainly have my words on repeat today."

"You said I should brand your words into my soul, to memorize them all," she added helpfully.

Leo dropped his face to his hands, inhaling hard through his fingers. "So I did. But you *lied to your Amish aunt.* What's going to happen when she tells your parents you're married?"

"She can't," Esther said, unconcerned.

"Because she doesn't have a phone?" he asked.

"There's a community phone, at the pole." She pointed behind him. "But it doesn't matter. My parents are in Haiti for the next four months. Mission work."

He blinked at her. "Your parents are in Haiti?"

She nodded.

Her parents were out of the country? "You're alone?"

She shook her head.

"Who do you have?"

She pointed to the center of his chest. He sank into a chair. The first licks of flame were beginning to give off some heat. Leo shuddered and had immediate regrets when his shoulder awoke and began to throb. A groan leaked out and Esther sprang into action.

"Come on, you need to rest. I'll stoke up the fire and get some food for us," she said.

"You haven't slept all night," he said, but he allowed her to pull him out of the chair and down the hall to a small bedroom. She peeled back the covers and held them, indicating he should slip inside. He wanted to argue, but the bed looked so inviting, the mattress so soft.

He eased into it with another groan. Esther pulled the covers up to his chin and perched on the edge of the bed. Her hand smoothed over his forehead, exactly as his mother might have done, if she'd ever been the motherly sort. He had a vague flicker of recollection about the touch. Maybe his grandmother had done it once a long time ago. Or maybe it was written into the heart of every man to yearn for a touch like that—so soothing, so tender, so filled with care. He closed his eyes and leaned into it. She skimmed her palm along the side of his face, her thumb sliding over his cheekbone.

"You should get some sleep," he made himself utter, suddenly remembering anew she'd been up all night.

"I'm fine, Leo. I need to see to the fire and make food."

He wanted to argue, to tell her she should go to sleep, cuddled up beside him so he could keep her safe and she could keep him warm. It was cold in the room, so cold. Esther was the only warm thing, her hand so soothing and hot. She shifted, adding another quilt on top of him. The weight was so heavy. It pulled him under. He fought it, tried to stay awake, to focus on her hand, her scent. *Vanilla,* he thought, and then the darkness came for him, dragging him under once more.

*H*e woke to darkness, in the room this time. He'd slept the day away, not the first time it happened. But this time he hadn't meant to; this time he had someone in his care and keeping. He sat up quickly and had immediate regrets when his head swam, his shoulder on fire.

He stumbled from the bedroom and down the hall to the kitchen/sitting area. On the stove sat a pot of soup and a loaf of homemade bread. Esther sat in a chair, twirling her braid in her fingers. "Hi, Leo. How are you feeling?"

Leo blinked, trying hard to take it all in. The room was dark, save for an old-fashioned lantern that gave off a surprising amount of soft, glowing light.

"I don't know. How long was I out that time?" he asked.

"Six hours."

"Six." He sat down hard at one of the kitchen chairs. Unlike the main house, this room only had two.

"You must be hungry," Esther said. She rose and began ladling soup into bowls. She set one before him and sliced the bread thickly before spreading a generous layer of butter on it. Leo hadn't realized he was hungry before this moment, but now he was starved. Saliva filled his dry mouth. He swallowed, fighting his gag reflex.

"Did your aunt make this?" he asked, already guessing the answer.

"No, I did," Esther said. She dished her own food and sat down beside him. She picked up her spoon and set it down when he remained staring at her. "What?"

"Aren't you supposed to pray?"

She gave him her amused smile. "If you'd like." She reached for his hand and said a soft and sweet little prayer. Leo picked up his spoon and tried to concentrate on his food, but inside he felt like he'd been raked over broken glass.

"What's wrong with you?" Esther said after a few minutes of heavy silence.

"I've been shot," he said.

"That's not what's wrong. It's something else. I've never seen you this uncomfortable before. You keep staring around the house like you smell a decaying possum hidden in the walls. Do you not like it here? We could try to find somewhere else." She frowned, and he realized she thought it was about her when, really, it was about him.

"No," he said. He couldn't reach for her with his left hand, so he set down his spoon, crossed it over his bowl, and took her hand. "Esther, listen, this is the perfect hiding spot. No one could find us here, really. It was genius to think of it."

"Then what is it?" she asked, staring up at him with big, worried eyes.

By the lantern light, she looked even younger and more innocent. "You're *Amish*," he said.

"Mennonite," she corrected.

"Still, it's…" He let her go and swiped a weary hand over his face, frustrated. "I knew you were innocent, knew you were naïve, but this…Esther, do you know the things I've done? What I've become? Who I am?"

"Who?" she said, her tone soft and gentle.

"The opposite of all this," he said, gesturing around them with his free hand. "You're so *pure*. I don't think I was ever this untouched, even when I was a newborn baby." He tore off a piece of bread, bread she'd made from scratch with her own hands and baked in a wood-stove, and shoved it in his mouth.

"Leo," Esther said, regarding him with a serious expression. "I'm still me, and you're still you. Nothing has changed."

"No, nothing has changed because this is always how it was." He had almost forgotten, almost allowed himself to set aside the differences between them and believe they could care for each other as more than impersonal coworkers, that they could be friends, real friends, the sort he hadn't had since he was a kid, if even then. Esther had started to feel like she was family, like she was his. But who was he kidding? This was her family, her *Amish* family; this was where she belonged. Not with a broken down old drunk like him.

"Leo, hey," she said, ducking low to make eye contact. His eyes had been circling the room like a panicky bunny. She made him focus on her, holding his gaze in an iron grip. "Eat your food."

He tore off another piece of bread, following it with a bite of soup and then another. Soon he'd eaten two bowls of soup, three pieces of bread, and two glasses of lemonade—lukewarm lemonade. No ice for the Amish, apparently. And when he was done he took a deep breath and felt better, the momentary panic forgotten.

"I'm sorry," he muttered, now staring at the scarred oak table. It looked ancient. He wondered how many *Dawdys* had owned it.

"It's been a long week," Esther said, squeezing the back of his neck as she eased past him to wash the dishes.

"Indoor plumbing," he remarked when she turned on the tap and water came out.

"Allowances are made for *Dawdys*. The toilet works, and there's a gas water heater, too," Esther said.

Leo breathed a sigh of relief. Electricity he could do without, no problem. But he hadn't been looking forward to that outhouse. "Mind if I shower?"

"I was about to insist on it. You stink, Leo."

He chuckled and stood, turning for the bathroom. Impulsively he pivoted back to the kitchen, to where Esther stood at the sink, her back to him. He rested his hand on her hip and leaned down to kiss her cheek. "Thank you for supper, wife." He said the last word flippantly, to tease her. It came out in a croak and a lead weight settled on his chest.

Either Esther didn't notice or she pretended not to because she merely leaned against him for the briefest flicker and said, "You're welcome," in a normal and congenial tone.

His other hand reached out, as if to pull her against him again. He imagined pressing his face to her neck, inhaling her signature vanilla scent. She would tip her head to the side, close her eyes, and say, *"Leo,"* and then…

He blinked, and the vision faded. He backstepped one space away, then again, until finally he found the strength to turn, walk down the hall, and lock himself in the bathroom.

CHAPTER 14

After soup, bread, lemonade, a shower, and his six-hour nap, Leo felt like a new creation. His shoulder still hurt like demon fire, but it was a feeling he could ignore. The post-blood loss exhaustion had been much worse, but now it appeared to be over. He emerged into the warm and cozy living room clean and refreshed in all the ways. Esther sat staring into the fire, looking drowsy. He wondered if things would be weird with her, but he should have known better. She seemingly had no idea what had almost happened, how close he'd come to giving in to the odd temptation a half hour ago.

She sat in the side chair, her feet propped on an ottoman. Leo sat on the settee and studied her. "Have you slept yet?"

She shook her head, snapping out of her trance to smile at him.

"Why not?"

"I was busy," she said, shrugging one shoulder, her fingers twining in her braid.

"The shower's free," he said.

Her smile widened. "Are you saying I stink, Leo?"

"You're still covered in my blood," he noted, pointing to the stain of his blood on her shoulder where she'd cradled him against her.

"Oh," she said, looking down with a flinch, her face pinching with the reminder.

"Are you okay?" he asked.

"Yes, I'm fine," she said. She stood and brushed by him. A minute later the shower started. A short time after that she emerged from the bathroom, bringing the scent of lavender soap with her. Now Leo was the one staring into the fire, lulled by the heat, by the gentle pop and crack of burning wood. *This is nice,* he thought. Someday he should have a place with a wood burning fireplace. It was the sort of warmth that seeped into the bones, much more than the modern forced air of his apartment.

Esther sat on the floor in front of the stove and began doing something with her hands. It took him a moment to realize she was combing her hair. At long last, the braid was gone. Her hair was free and, as he'd suspected, hung in a glorious sheet down to her hips.

"How do you comb it when it's so long?" he whispered, his fascinated gaze unwavering on her progress.

"Very carefully," she said, sounding pained. It was no easy task for her small arms to try and skim through the layers. Leo nudged her with his foot and motioned her closer. She eased backwards until she bumped the edge of the settee. He leaned forward, took the comb, and began using it with his good hand. Even so, it was a workout. Her hair must weigh a ton.

"Doesn't this give you a headache?" he asked.

"Every day," she said. Her eyes were glazed as if she were enjoying the sensation of his fingers in her hair as much as he was. He set aside the comb and began sliding his fingers over her scalp. She closed her eyes and fastened her arms around his legs to keep from keeling over. "I should let Amelia cut it," she added in a whisper.

"Don't," he said, sounding pained. "Who's the long-haired goddess?"

"Aphrodite," she supplied.

"Right, that one. You look like her."

"Have all the women you've been with had long hair?" she asked.

"I can't remember," he said honestly. He couldn't remember any of their faces or features. He picked up the comb again and resumed sorting her hair. When he finished, he gave the comb back to her. She clutched it to her chest and rested her head on his knee, eyes closed.

"Go to bed," he said, squeezing her shoulder.

"Can't," she murmured.

"Why not?"

"You're sitting on it."

"What? Go to bed, an actual bed," he commanded.

She turned to peer up at him. "Leo, there's only one."

Reality dawned. The house was tiny, too tiny for more than one bedroom. He was a dunce. "You take the bed," he commanded, his hand smoothing over her shoulder again.

She shook her head. "You're injured. You need your rest."

"I've had my rest, and I'm perfectly comfortable here. Your turn to sleep."

"No, the bed is for guests," she said, turning stubborn.

"We're both guests," he reminded her.

"But…"

He pressed his finger to her lips. "As the head of this household, I'm telling you to take the bed." He expected her to argue, mostly because he was joking. In his experience it never worked to pull rank on a woman. But once again he forgot Esther wasn't like most women. She took him at his word and, meekly, stood and walked into the bedroom.

Leo remained staring at the fire, trying not to feel disappointed and alone, trying not to feel anything at all. He added more wood to the fire a few times until, eventually, he fell into a restless, uncomfortable slumber.

A few hours later, he awoke to panicked whimpers, Esther's, to be exact. He bolted upright, disoriented. He stood blinking in the darkness, trying to remember where he was, where she was. She whimpered again and he headed in her direction, imagining the worst, an assailant, a rapist, a murderer.

But when he reached the room, Esther was in bed alone, thrashing the covers off, panic building. If he didn't wake her soon, she would likely start screaming. He eased forward and touched her arm. She yelped and rolled away from him. He put his hand out again, trying to soothe her. But again his touch had the opposite effect. This time when she flailed, she belted him in the ribs, only a few inches below his injured shoulder. Leo saw stars. For a moment he thought he might throw up or pass out, but Esther became increasingly agitated. He did the only thing he could think of; he climbed into the bed and lay on top of her, smashing her flat beneath him.

Instantly, she went still. For a moment he feared he'd killed her, so much smaller was she than he. But about thirty seconds after the thrashing stopped, she spoke, her voice small and afraid. "Leo?"

"Shh, I'm here. You were having a bad dream."

She nodded, sniffling, and then it was as if a dam broke and she started to cry in earnest, great heaving sobs that wracked her body. He started to roll away. She clutched his shirt. "Don't, don't move. I need the pressure to pull myself together."

"It's okay to cry," he told her.

"Then why don't you ever do it?" she asked.

"Who says I don't?"

"You don't, I would know."

"How would you know?" he asked.

"Because it would make you feel better, and you're miserable," she said, ending on a breathless little quaver.

"Can't argue with that," he said, but at the moment he didn't feel miserable. It seemed he liked squishing her as much as she liked being squished. At the moment, he felt so…what? Peaceful, perhaps. Even though a woman sobbed an inch away, beneath him, he was aware it was a release of all the stress she'd stored the last few days and not some deeper sort of trauma. Not like him, whose trauma went so deep there seemed to be no end to it.

"I was so afraid," she trembled.

"I know," he soothed. His hands were useless, trapped as they were beneath him. He had only his words. "You did so good, and it's okay, it's all okay. You're fine."

"I wasn't afraid for me. I was afraid for you." She shuddered hard, making him shudder in response. Pain rippled through him, but it was almost cathartic, another purge of bottled emotion. He'd been afraid, too. It felt good to let go of a little of that fear.

"I'm going to roll off you now," he said, and she whimpered, a small little wounded animal sound. "So I can hold you," he added. He rolled to his bad side, wincing. It landed on the soft bed, not as painful as he'd thought it would be. His good arm reached out and gathered Esther close, pressing her against him. And then he could soothe her properly, using his hand to smooth up and down her neck, over her ear, her shoulder her back. "You're okay, *we're* okay. It's going to be all right."

She nodded, nestling against him, fitting her nose into its sacred spot, and Leo admitted it was what he'd been waiting for. She had been content with being smashed, but he wasn't. He had needed and wanted to hold her and feel her respond in kind, surrendering herself to his care.

"Don't go back to the couch," she pled.

He didn't bother to tell her it hadn't crossed his mind. "All right," he said, as if conceding to some overlarge request. She sat up and pulled the blankets over both or them. The bedroom was cold, but Esther was warm. She nestled back into her spot, winding her fingers in his shirt. He did the same to her hair, threading his fingers in the mass, his thumb sliding over the silky strands.

"Leo," she murmured, her voice sluggish with repressed sleep.

"Mm."

"Anam cara."

A minute later, her soft, even breathing told him she was asleep. Careful not to wake her, Leo stretched to the nightstand and picked up his phone. It had enough battery to flick awake and look up the word. *Anam cara: A person with whom you can share your deepest thoughts and feelings; a soul friend.*

*L*eo woke the next morning, hands outstretched, grasping at the empty bed beside him. It took him a groggy moment to remember why, or rather who he reached for. He sat up and took stock. Shoulder: painful but livable. Room: freezing. Bed: lonely. Leo: pathetic. Esther: most likely gainfully employed caring for him in some capacity.

Gingerly, he peeled back the covers and stumbled to the kitchen. Esther sat in front of the fire, coaxing it back to life. Her hands were cupped around her mouth and she blew, her lips making a gentle whooshing sound. Her hair was still down, surrounding her face and shoulders in a black cloud. Leo's gut clenched, and he couldn't understand why. It wasn't a lustful feeling. So far in his life, that was the sum total of his experience with women. He had no idea what to do with soft and easy affection, the sort that made him feel monstrously protective and cared for all at once. In the past his relationships had been usurious, almost a barter system. He and women had a mutual understanding: he only gave as much as he took which, in the scheme of things, wasn't much.

"The fire's being stubborn," Esther whispered. He didn't realize she was aware of his presence because she hadn't looked at him. She did so now, pushing her hair out of her face with the back of her hand. He smiled at her, for no other reason than he liked her and she was pleasant to look at. Dawn's early glow was the only light in the room, giving everything a rosy hue.

"I'll see to the fire," he said.

"Your shoulder," she said, biting her lip as her gaze settled worriedly on his arm.

"It's okay, I have another one," he said, flexing his good shoulder. He walked across the tiny room and lowered himself beside her. She started to stand, and Leo felt bereft. "Don't go."

"I have to make coffee and breakfast," she said, but she sank back beside him.

"You know I can't digest food this early. It's still practically the middle of the night," he said.

She smiled. "The farm's been up forever. They probably think we're lazy." She sighed. "We're going to have to venture out today."

"Why?" he asked.

She wove her fingers together and held them up for his inspection. "The Amish are like this. Community is a big deal. Not a lot of loners here."

"Yikes for me," he said.

"You're not a loner," she replied.

"We're loners together," he said. The fire began to take off. He eased his arm around Esther and she nestled closer, her hair a giant barrier between them. He began to see why she always kept it contained as he pushed a piece out of his mouth. He attempted to tuck it behind her ear, but it sprang free.

"That's not what I meant. Even without me, you're not a loner. You pretend to be, but you're not. People like you."

"Of course they don't."

"Of course they do," she said. Her nose nuzzled into its spot and she closed her eyes, resting her head on him. He slipped both arms around her and pulled her snug against him.

"Esther, people don't like me. I'm a train wreck."

She shook her head, stubbornly, he thought. "People see all the goodness inside you, all the kindness and warmth you pretend aren't there. Why do you do that?" Her eyes opened. She pulled back to inspect him.

He frowned. "What are you talking about? I'm a grumpy screwup."

She shook her head.

His frown deepened to a scowl. "You don't know."

"You don't think I know? Who knows you better than I do?"

He opened his mouth but nothing came out. "You don't know everything," he muttered at last. "There's a lot you don't know. A lot."

"Do you think when you tell me it's going to change my opinion of you?" she asked.

He opened his mouth and closed it again. There was nothing he could tell her that would make her see him differently, he realized. He wasn't certain if the thought was comforting or terrifying. "But you're

Amish," he said at last, and Esther giggled, a bubble of laughter unlike anything he'd ever heard from her. She pressed both hands over her mouth, trying to push it back down. He peeled them away and she laughed out loud, pressing her face to his chest to muffle the sound.

"You've really got to get over it," she said when she had herself back under control.

"I don't think I can," he said seriously, his thumb caressing her earlobe. She was so pure, and he was so not. They sat in cozy silence while the fire warmed them. At some point Esther had eased into his lap, half her hair tossed over his wounded shoulder like a macabre bandage.

"Trouvaille," Esther murmured.

"My phone's dead," he murmured in return.

"A lucky and unexpected find," she said.

"Am I your pot of gold, Esther?"

"Gold means nothing to me, Leo. You're my best friend."

A little tremble of fear and pain shuddered through him. Being alone, aloof, and untethered was so much safer, so much easier. Caring about someone meant he could lose them. A part of him, a big part, desperately wanted to retreat, retreat, retreat. But he couldn't. He had nowhere to go, and Esther needed him. "We need to get new clothes."

"There's a Wal-Mart a half hour away," she said.

"No good, they have cameras."

"Thrift store in town," she said, suppressing a yawn.

"You could go back to bed. I won't tell. We could *both* go back to bed." The thought of crawling in bed again, snuggled down with Esther, sounded better than anything in recent memory.

Someone knocked on the door. "Too late," Esther said, pushing away from him to answer.

CHAPTER 15

Leo rode in a carriage once, when he was still young and naïve enough to try and impress girls. He'd paid eighty bucks for a horse to drag them around a park while his date texted selfies to her friend the entire time.

That experience did nothing to prepare him for being chauffeured in an Amish buggy by Esther's silent cousin. The boy was fourteen, if he was a day.

"Shouldn't he be in school?" Leo whispered to Esther.

"He's done with school," she replied.

"How old is he?" he asked.

Esther studied the boy. "No idea. Must be past eighth grade, though. That's when they quit going to school."

"You don't know how old your cousin is?" he asked.

"You realize I have about a hundred cousins," she said, unconcerned. "You're Jacob, right?" she said to the boy.

He gave her a curt nod, his eyes never leaving the road. He didn't have to watch, the horse seemed to know the way. But his ruddy cheeks said he wasn't used to strangers.

Jacob dropped them at the thrift store and sped off, as much as horse and buggy could speed. "How will we get home?" Leo asked.

"We'll figure something out," Esther said, unconcerned. Leo stood in the middle of the street, staring. He felt like he'd been dropped on another planet, or maybe another century. Esther took his hand and tugged him forward. They entered the store and Esther headed for the Amish section, homemade shirts, skirts, and dresses. Leo retrieved her and pulled her back.

"Something different," he said.

She scanned the interior of the store with something like panic. "I have no idea what people wear." Leo couldn't help, he was equally clueless about women's fashion. Across the store, he spotted two teenagers who looked like they were hoping to find vintage Prada and about to be royally disappointed. He led Esther to them. They glanced up warily, causing him to wonder if they were skipping school. What was it with children in these parts and their lack of devotion to school? Little deviants.

"Hi, my wife is playing this game with her sister to see who can assemble the best thrift store wardrobe. Our honor is at stake, but we're both kind of clueless at this stuff. Would you guys mind helping her out?" He pulled Esther forward and shoved her at them.

They scanned her up and down and glanced back at him, smiling now. "Sure."

"Thanks," he said, smiling in return. "I'll be over there." He pointed to the men's section and eased away. The girls had already taken Esther in hand and were pulling clothes off the rack for her. They looked like the kind of girls who had their own YouTube channel for makeup tutorials. Satisfied she was in capable hands, he turned his attention to his own clothing, grabbing some denim, flannels, and hoodies without really noticing what was on them, along with a baseball cap. He had planned to slip to the dollar store and buy underpants, but the thrift shop had a selection of new ones, along with socks. *Trouvaille,* he thought, smiling.

Esther was nowhere in sight when he finished making his selections. He felt a momentary surge of panic until he heard giggles coming from the dressing room. He pictured Esther standing between two giggling teenagers and felt a moment of worry. Were they making fun of her? She would have no idea how to relate to two teenage girls, probably even less than he would. Maybe it was a mistake to foist her on them. He sat and stewed for a while as the giggles grew louder and more excited until at last he couldn't take it anymore and decided he should intervene. He had just gripped the handles of the chair he sat in when the dressing room curtain was ripped open. The girls stood behind Esther and pushed her forward, the proverbial lamb being led to slaughter. Only she didn't look like a lamb. She looked…well, she looked normal. Gone were the homemade ankle-length dresses he was used to. In their place, she wore a form-fitting sweater and a pair of jeans, highlighting her slight, yet curvy, figure. They had also taken her hair out of its braid and arranged it in some sort of messy topknot. He took a step forward, squinting. "Are you wearing makeup?"

She nodded. "Lola said it brings out my eyes."

"So it does," he agreed.

"She looks hot, doesn't she? Tell her she looks hot," one of the girls commanded.

"Hot," Leo said uncomfortably. Amish Esther, hot. Huh. Awkward.

The girls hugged Esther, and she returned it before fishing in her pocket and giving them each a twenty. "Thank you, girls. Buy yourselves something fun."

"Aw, man, thanks, Es. Awesome." They stared at the money with awe. Leo remembered being that age, when twenty bucks felt like a windfall. Who was he kidding? His finances were so abysmal it still felt like a windfall.

They walked to the counter and he felt abashed when Esther pulled out more money and paid for their purchases. Why was he so ridiculously bad with his money? He was a grown man, for goodness sake, one who'd been gainfully employed since becoming an adult. Shouldn't he have more to show for it than a crummy car and lousy apartment? At what point in life would he stop making excuses and start to get it together?

He had no debt, the only point in his favor. The marines had paid for his college education, saving him from loans. And he didn't carry a balance on his credit card. It was probably the one positive thing he did in his life, paying off his card every month. But he had no savings, nothing to call his own. Why did he still rent? Why hadn't he bought a house by now?

You don't deserve a house. The little voice popped up every time he considered biting the bullet and taking on a mortgage. Leo's spirits fell. Why did he think himself capable of home ownership? That was for normal people, good people, solid people like Esther and her family. Ridge and Maggie. Families, people who made the world better by being in it. Leo was a liability, had always been a liability. His earliest memories were of trying to stay out of his mother's way, trying to stay quiet so he didn't upset her. He had started taking care of himself far before other kids, making boxes of still crunchy macaroni and cheese for supper when he was eight, getting himself up and dressed for school, buying groceries so he'd have something to eat when he was a teen. How could a guy like him ever belong in the suburban world of minivans and soccer moms?

Esther linked her arm with his as they headed back onto the street. "What's next?"

He stopped short and scanned the town. What was next? He had no idea. Esther, sensing his dismay, took over. "A picnic," she suggested.

"A picnic," he agreed, glad to have some direction. They walked to a deli at the end of the street and ordered two lunches to go. They carried them to a park across the street and sat down. Leo sat still, staring at Esther while she arranged their food, fussing over it like usual. "Did you come here a lot when you were a kid?"

"Yes. My parents are still close to their families, despite leaving the Amish community." She sighed and stared off into the distance.

"What?" He wasn't actually hungry yet, not after the massive breakfast her aunt had foisted on them, hand delivered by yet another cousin.

"Nothing, I…I never fit."

"How so?" he asked.

"I loved learning, always. I was a voracious reader, couldn't get enough. The Amish, they think education leads to pride. It's why they quit school after eighth grade. To them my thirst for knowledge looked like a thirst for pride."

"You're the least proud person I know," he said. It was true; Esther gave no thought to self.

"I didn't fit in other ways," she said.

"What ways?" he asked, suddenly insatiably curious. How had they worked together for the past few months and he hadn't asked so many fundamental things about her?

"The purpose of a woman's life here is to get married and make babies." Her cheeks flushed a soft shade of pink. She opened a mustard packet and added it to her sandwich to give herself something to do.

"And you wanted a career?" he guessed.

She nodded.

"Don't you want to get married someday and have babies?" he asked.

"That's not for me," she said.

"Why not?" he asked.

"Because I'm different."

"Being different doesn't preclude you from being a wife and mother, if you want," he said.

She swallowed hard and shook her head. He sat up. "Esther, what's this about?"

"I'm not like other women, other people," she said softly.

"So? Who says you have to be a carbon copy to be worthwhile?" His tone was irritable. Esther was the best and kindest person he knew.

She shook her head, eyes still on her sandwich.

"Hey," he said, tipping her face to his. "Who made you feel this way? So unworthy?"

"Everybody," she whispered, and then amended, "Everybody but you."

"Maybe no one knows you the way I do," he said.

"If that's true, why don't you believe me when I say the same about you?" she countered.

He frowned and dropped his hand. "We're not talking about me. We're talking about you. You can be a wife or mother or have a career. You can be anything you want because you are amazing and worthwhile, and anyone who makes you feel otherwise can deal with me." He reached for his sandwich and took an angry bite.

"Ditto," she said, her delicate bite stark contrast to his wolverine one.

He rolled his eyes, but his cheeks were too stuffed to make a reply.

"What do you want, Leo?"

He shrugged. She poked him. "If my secret dream is to be normal, to be like other women, what's yours?"

He chewed and swallowed, pushing the food down a gullet that was suddenly dry. What did he want? He had never asked himself that question before. His entire life felt like he'd been in survival mode. It was hard to want things when he was doing his best to get through each day. But maybe if he had a goal, something to work toward, he would begin to know how to work toward it. "I guess I'd like to have a house. In the country. All my own. With a wood burning stove." He glanced at her to see how that was received. In his head he knew she wouldn't laugh at him, but he knew her so well. He'd be able to tell if she thought it was stupid. She looked thoughtful, though. Rather dreamy.

"*Saudade.*"

He shrugged. Without his phone, he had no way to look up her words.

"It's Portuguese, a melancholy longing for something you've never had. And really, Leo, I think there's nothing better you could long for than a home."

He swallowed hard and looked away. *Home.* The word had never had a positive connotation for him, but he wanted it to. He wanted a peaceful, happy, relaxing place to ease his many wounds. Could it be possible to heal everything that was wrong with him? Lately he felt like maybe it was. Esther's words had created some kind of patching effect, a spackle over his raw pieces, and he wanted more of it. More healing, more wholeness. How would it feel to look in the mirror and like the person who stared back at him? Leo had no idea. It was why he had no mirrors.

"I want that for you," she continued. "I'll help however I can. We'll think of a plan. You can have my money." She perked up, eyes brightening.

"I don't want your money," he said.

"Houses are expensive," she reminded him.

"I know, but…it has to be from me. Does that make sense? It has to be something I do."

"Yes, I suppose," she said, sitting back. "At least let me make your curtains. I'm really good at sewing, and curtains are expensive."

Leo laughed. Right now buying a house seemed like an insur-mountable challenge. He had to get his life in order and save for a down payment, but such was Esther's absolute faith in his ability to do so that she was already mentally sewing his curtains. "Everyone should have a friend like you, Esther."

She deflated a little. "You're the only one who believes that, Leo."

"Then everyone else is wrong," he said, tearing off another bite of his sandwich.

"You're a feral eater lately. Kind of terrifying," she said.

He wagged his brows at her and tore off another bite.

She laughed and took a delicate nibble of her own sandwich.

CHAPTER 16

"What were the girls giggling about when they were getting you ready?" he asked. They hadn't seemed like they were making fun of her; they had seemed like they liked her.

"Oh, I was telling them a story."

"What story?" he asked. She made him laugh, but seemingly nobody else. He was almost a little bit jealous of her newfound friendship with two random teenagers, and how sad was that?

"They wanted to know about us, how we met and fell in love," she said.

"And what did you tell them?" he asked, curiosity now overriding his jealousy. The sun was warm and cozy, his belly full, and suddenly he was sleepy. He lay down on his back in the grass and tried to stare up at her, but the sun was too bright. Instead he patted the space beside him and she lay down next to him. They were parallel bars, stretched out, absorbing the sun.

"Obviously I had to lie," she said, her voice tinged with guilt.

"Obviously," he said. He reached for her hand, clasped it, and gave it a squeeze. "What lie did you come up with, super spy?"

She paused, then, "It was our story, just…embellished. I told them you picked me up from the airport and I felt…"

She paused again and he turned his head to face her. "What did you feel?"

She faced him. "*Koi no yokan.*"

"What's that?"

"It's Japanese. It means the extraordinary sense upon meeting someone with whom you will one day fall in love."

"Oh," he said.

She smiled. "They liked that, thought it was very romantic."

"So it is. And when did we fall in love?"

"It was a gradual process. First we were strangers, then we became friends, and then…"

"And then," he prompted when she paused again. He wondered if she had drawn out the story suspensefully for her first audience. If so, he bet they ate it up.

"And then we realized our lives are so interconnected we could never untangle. We already belong. What was left but to make it official?"

His heart thundered…was she actually saying…did she mean…?

"Also they said you're hot a bunch of times. That probably accounted for the giggles." She turned her face away, toward the sun, and closed her eyes.

"I've reached that age where being called hot by fifteen year olds is more creepy than flattering," he said, turning his face to the sun also. He tried to keep his eyes open, but it was too intense. He squeezed them tightly closed instead.

"I wouldn't know the feeling. I've never been one of the pretty girls."

He sighed, hating the way she made such sad statements with so little emotion. "Esther, you're very pretty." He gave her hand a squeeze for emphasis.

"You only think that because you're my friend. You see me through a different filter. When we first met, you didn't think so."

"Not true, I did."

She paused again and this time sat up to stare down at him. "Did you, really? Or are you trying to boost my self-image? Because I'll know if you're lying."

Her hair was already popping free of its confinement. He reached up to tuck it behind her ear with no success. "No, you would never know if I'm lying because it's what I do for a living. But I happen to be telling the truth. I thought you were very pretty in a wholesome way."

"In a wholesome way. What does that mean?"

"The women I go out with, they're different than you."

"They're pretty," she said.

He hooked an arm around her and dragged her close so she was half-lying on his chest. "Shh, listen while I try to explain. There are hard people in the world and soft people. People like me, like the women I date, we're the hard ones. We were born fighting a battle. People like you, soft people, have other people to fight for you. Do you understand?"

"Yes, except you're wrong."

"Which part?" he asked.

"You're soft. A big, soft softie." She turned her head, pressing her ear to his heart.

He chuckled. "Uh, no. Wrong. I've never sustained a relationship in my life, and I've ended them all in the cruelest way possible, ghosting out of women's lives like they were worthless. A woman starts to cling, I disappear."

"He said to the woman now clinging to his chest like a baby sloth."

He rolled his eyes. "I can't leave you. You're the job."

"Okay, Leo," she said easily.

He sat up, wincing when his shoulder yanked painfully. "Stop. Stop getting attached to me. I'm going to hurt you. Do you not understand that? I'm going to let you down, disappoint you, break your heart."

"Okay."

He pressed his hands to his temples. "Stop saying okay. It's not okay. I'm going to destroy you. You're far too tender and naïve. Pairing me with you was like siccing a wolf on a baby chick. You never even had a chance."

She regarded him seriously a moment and then burst into a fit of completely unexpected giggles. Leo growled, got to his feet, and stormed away, her tinkling laughter echoing behind him.

He walked far and fast, until his shoulder stung so badly his eyes burned. And then he returned and sat down beside her. She was quiet now, staring mutely at the horizon. He stared, too. They both sat perfectly still, staring at nothing.

"There's nowhere to go. I can't get away from you," he said at last.

"I know." She slung an arm companionably over his shoulders and gave them a squeeze.

"I'm going to hurt you," he warned. "I'm going to break your heart."

"Okay, Leo."

His sigh sounded frustrated, but really he felt at peace, the same oozing sense of peace he always felt in her presence. They sat in silence a few more minutes and then she rubbed a little circle on his back. "We should go. You need a nap."

He scowled, wanting to argue that he didn't need a nap. He wasn't a toddler. But he yawned and ruined it. Suddenly, he was exhausted. Esther stood, clasped his hand, and pulled him up. Their hands remained clasped while they walked.

"Are we going to walk all the way back?" he asked. It was a few miles to her aunt and uncle's house, on a hilly country road. He was exhausted thinking about it.

"Nah, we'll catch a ride with someone. There must be a cousin around here somewhere." She scanned the area, caught sight of someone across the road, and quickly faced away pressing her nose to Leo's chest. Reflexively, his arm made a protective little cage around her shoulders, drawing her closer.

"What is it?" he asked, senses instantly attuned to danger. He hadn't brought his gun, mostly because he was almost out of ammo. He hadn't expected to feel threatened in this tiny Amish burg, but now that he did he felt naked without it. What kind of spy leaves home without his gun? *The dead kind, that's who.*

"Nothing, shh. Maybe he didn't see us."

She had never told him to shh before. It must be serious. But before he could question her further, the man was crossing the street and standing in front of them.

"Esther?"

He didn't look the same as all the Amish men around them. For one thing he wasn't wearing a black jacket over his shirt. But it was clearly a homemade shirt, and he wore suspenders. Not trendy hipster suspenders, but old man suspenders, even though he couldn't have been out of his twenties. He was tall and sort of doofy looking with a really bad bowl haircut.

Esther cleared her throat and peeled her nose out of Leo's chest. She pasted on an unconvincing smile and took a breath. "Ruben. Hi. This is…" she motioned helplessly to Leo.

"I'm Leo, Esther's husband."

Ruben blinked at him, then turned his gaze on Esther. "You… you're married?"

"It came about very quickly. There wasn't time to…" she glanced away, biting her lip. "Sorry."

"Another cousin?" Leo asked, preemptively knowing it wasn't. Esther wouldn't have reacted that way to family.

"No, Ruben is, um, was…"

"The man she was going to marry," Ruben said.

"You were engaged?" Leo asked.

"No," Esther said, while Ruben said, "As good as."

"What does that mean, as good as?" Leo asked.

"It was intended, if never specified. For years." Ruben ran a hand through his doofy hair, upending it. Leo supposed he should feel sorry for him, but something held him back, and it wasn't because Ruben sounded jealous or proprietary. He would have expected that. It was more the incredulity. Somehow Leo got the sense that Esther had been taken for granted by this man, that she was a fallback, someone he always assumed would be there.

"Well, I guess you should have specified," Leo said, easing his hand up to swipe his thumb on Esther's neck. Ruben followed the touch, his eyes slamming down in a puzzled frown.

"How'd you meet?" Ruben asked.

"Work," Esther said. "Leo's my," she paused and cleared her throat as his finger swiped over her neck again, "handler."

"What's that mean, handler?" Ruben asked.

"We're partners, basically. Good cop and bad cop," Leo said.

Ruben tipped his head like a disconcerted collie. "I thought you worked for some accounting firm."

"Yes, but it's a government accounting firm. Lots of secrets," Leo said, pressing his index finger to his lips in emphasis.

Ruben stared off into the distance, arms crossed, flummoxed. "Do you need a ride or something?"

"Absolutely," Leo volunteered before Esther could turn him down. He had no idea why he wanted to prolong the awkward misery of this encounter, except for his extreme annoyance with Ruben's reaction to Esther. It would be one thing if he were heartbroken, but it was more like someone bought his prize heifer at the county fair, the one he'd had his eye on. There was no love in his eyes when he looked at Esther. In fact, Leo thought he saw a little bit of meanness, of superiority. Unless Leo was wrong, Ruben was a bully. A fact confirmed when he opened his mouth and spoke to Esther again.

"You look different." His eyes scanned her up and down. The way he said "different" made it sound like, "horrible." Esther pressed her lips together and glanced away, wounded, but Leo was having none of that.

"Amazing," he intercepted. "I finally talked her out of the braid." He meant it, Esther did look amazing, but it was more than the new clothes and the less-confining hairstyle. She was more open now, as if she was finally coming into her own, getting to know and like who she was. It was an amazing thing to see, to be a part of. Leo was always the one responsible for tearing a woman down. He had never been part of building one up before. But Esther was blossoming, and it was due in part to his tutelage, forcing her out of her comfort zones. By doing things that frightened her, she grew more confident. Confidence was always sexy, even in a Mennonite, apparently.

They followed Ruben to a truck. Leo glanced at Esther in question. No horse and buggy? *Mennonite*, she mouthed, and he got caught up for a second staring at her mouth. Most women he'd been with knew how to work it, how to make the most of what they had, how to appeal to men. Esther had no idea, none whatsoever, that slowly mouthing a word caused him to stare at her mouth and ponder what else it could do. Her innocence was both captivating and terrifying. Leo had no desire to be the man to take it away, to break it, to ruin it forever. It was too much weight, too much responsibility. Then again, someone would be that man. What if it was someone worse? Someone like Ruben who would bumble and bully it away, would terrify and traumatize her?

She vaulted up into the middle seat. Wearily, Leo climbed up beside her. He would have to reach out and pull the door closed. He hesitated; the action was going to hurt. Esther, preempting him without a word, leaned over him, far out the door, and pulled it closed.

Leo swallowed hard and turned his face to the window, willing away his body's reaction to her. *Smells good: check. Looks good: check. Feels good: double check. Off limits for all eternity: CHECK, CHECK, CHECK.*

Esther, unaware as always, smoothed her hand over his leg and regarded him with a look of concern. He wondered what his face looked like at the moment, and if she would be convinced it was because his shoulder hurt. But of course she would be; she couldn't read his mind, a good thing for everyone. He forced a smile and took her hand, mostly to stop it from smoothing over his thigh.

"How long have you been married?" Ruben asked, resentment heavy in his tone. Or was it incredulity? Did he suspect not everything between them was on the up and up? Leo, a liar by nature, decided to field all questions.

"Not long, a couple of weeks. We probably should have waited until her parents returned from Haiti, but I couldn't stand it that long." He brought her hand to his lips and kissed it.

"What brings you for a visit?" Ruben asked.

"I'd never seen an Amish person in real life before," Leo volunteered. "Fascinating. And it's a bit of country life for us to explore.

Soon we need to decide if we want to buy a place in the city or live in the country." He turned his eyes to the window again, interestedly this time. It really was beautiful country. He'd hardly seen any of the United States, having spent so much of his career overseas. What would it be like to have a plot of land on one of these idyllic little roadways? "Maybe we should live here. I'm sure Esther would like to live close to family."

She gave him the side eye. *I don't think so,* she seemed to be saying.

"Eventually," he added. "When you've been away from home long enough to miss them. Also, babies. Women want to be near their families when they have babies." Where was all this coming from? He sounded like he had some idea of what he was talking about when, really, he had none. He had taken great care over the years to make certain he was never a father. What did he know about babies or families or commitment? *Nothing, absolutely nothing. You are alone, have always been alone, will always be alone.*

"I think you and I would both like to live far enough from family to have some autonomy," Esther interjected, possibly trying to restore a bit of reason to his runaway mouth. Country lanes. Babies. Family. Fantastical nonsense. But as he stared out the window, he could picture it, could see himself living in one of those houses, being one of those people. What was wrong with him? He touched his hand to his forehead. No fever. The delirium must be from something else.

"So your dad hasn't given his blessing," Ruben said, sounding pleased.

"In a manner of speaking," Esther replied

"In what manner?" Ruben asked.

"When he left me in the city, he left me in Leo's care," Esther said. Leo wondered if it was true. Hers had clearly been a patriarchal upbringing. She wouldn't have found it odd to transfer care of her wellbeing from her father to Leo. But had her father actually done that? Had he dropped his wholesome, innocent, untested daughter in the city, in the care of an unknown man, merely because he was a man? Leo felt white-hot shivers of rage on her behalf. He could have been a psycho, a murderer, he could have abused her, abandoned her, hurt her in every possible way. She would have been far better on her own than she would have been with some men he knew.

Esther gave him the side eye again, and he realized his jaw and fist were clenched, knuckles popping. Esther was worth more than everyone in her world seemed to realize. She was not a piece of property to be handed off and traded. Not a breeder, not a problem, not an oddity. Why did he seem to be the only person who saw her true worth?

He could almost hear her answer in his head. *Why am I the only person who is able to see yours?* His head swiveled to the window again. Was it possible? Was he worth more than he realized, more than everyone who had ever known him understood? Or, another possibility, did they merely bring out the best in each other? Like true partners should. Holmes and Watson. Leo and Esther. *It has a nice ring to it,* he admitted, his gaze fastened on another country lane.

CHAPTER 17

R uben stayed longer than Leo or Esther wanted, darting them
resentful, suspicious looks the entire time. Leo kept up the
pretense of being in love, hovering adoringly near Esther. It wasn't as
much of a stretch of his acting skills as he thought it might be. They
knew each other well, after so many weeks of working closely
together. He could read her face, usually knew what she thought,
understood what made her tick, what caused her to laugh or frown. In
short, he knew her better than he'd ever known anyone in his life, and
liked her better, too.

They ate supper with her family, her aunt, uncle, and more cousins
than Leo could name or count. They ate at their own table, but there
were so many people in the kitchen he didn't feel ostracized. And
there was so much food. Roast, bread, potatoes, vegetables, and
multiple pies for dessert.

Esther helped clean up while Leo asked Aaron questions about his
job. He was the first carpenter Leo had ever known in real life. He
gladly took Leo to his shop and showed him a few works in progress.
Leo was fascinated. He ran his hands over each piece and thought he
would probably never run out of questions. How would it feel to
make something with his hands? To build something, rather than

destroy?

Eventually he sensed Esther standing in the doorway. He turned, expecting to see the ubiquitous ankle-length dress and braid, momentarily forgetting she now wore jeans, her hair half up and half down in a messy bun gone wrong.

"Ready?" she asked.

He nodded. The sight of her had *not* knocked him temporarily breathless, it was merely the shock of seeing her in different clothes. With different hair. In a different place. *She's the same Esther,* he reassured himself, but his breath didn't come back. She held out her hand to him, and he took it, allowing himself to be led to the *Dawdy haus.* It was dark, but not cold. Probably one of the little cousins had been sent over to stoke the fire.

"Should we light the lantern, try to find something to do?" he asked, suppressing a yawn.

"No, we're exhausted. You shower, and then I'll take my turn." She checked the fire. Leo didn't argue, but he felt antsy. He showered, being careful to save hot water for her. The tank was small, too small for a luxuriously long soak. And Esther had all that hair to wash, miles and miles of it.

They passed each other in the hallway. Esther went into the bathroom and closed the door. Leo took a step toward the bedroom and stopped. Did it look presumptuous for him to go there? Like he thought he should be given the bed. Esther should be given the bed. Women should have the bed. He would take the settee. But she would insist he take the bed, he knew she would. And then they would bicker, growing more and more tired as they tried to one-up each other with good manners and self-lessness.

He dithered so long in the hallway that Esther finished. He glanced at her, eyes going to her hair, which was dry.

"I don't wash it every day, takes too long to comb and dry," she answered his unasked question.

"Ah, I see." He opened his mouth to ask her which she wanted, the bed or the couch, when she linked her arm with his and herded him toward the bedroom. She lifted the covers and slipped between them, then settled her gaze on him, waiting expectantly.

If he asked, it would make it seem like he thought it was a big deal for them to share the bed, which it wasn't. Totally. They were friends and nothing more, they'd established that. Esther was so innocent and clean she practically squeaked when she walked. It wasn't like that with her.

Resolved, he blew out a breath, climbed over her, and crawled into bed. It was not a king-size, this bed. Esther was small, but even so, they were pressed against each other, side to side.

"Are you in pain?" she asked.

"I'm okay." His shoulder hurt, but it was bearable. If he didn't think about it, he could almost forget, minus his limited range of motion. He wouldn't be able to handle man-to-man combat anytime soon, and that was beyond annoying. In his line of work, it could be deadly. Especially with Esther under his care. But they were in Amish country. What was the worst that could happen?

"What's wrong? You're all tense," she said.

He paused. "I've never slept with a woman before."

"Color me incredulous, Leo," she said, deadpan, and he snorted a laugh.

"I mean literally. I've never physically slept in a bed with a female for an entire night before."

She sat up, peering down at him. "I don't understand."

"When a woman and I have gotten everything we want from our time together, either she leaves or I do," he explained.

She blinked at him. "I didn't think that was possible." She lay back down.

"Didn't think what was possible?" he asked.

"Being with someone in that way without being in a relationship with them."

He blinked at the ceiling. Wow, just wow. So innocent. "Yep." That was all he was going to explain on that particular subject. Fortunately she didn't ask for any follow up. But now he was curious. "You've never been with a man that way, I take it." He knew it, down to his marrow. But after meeting Ruben, he needed to have it confirmed.

"Of course not," she said, her tone prim.

He smiled at the ceiling. They were quiet a few beats until she spoke again. "My mom showed me a book, when I started college. It had diagrams. It was the most disgusting thing I've ever seen in my life. When she left the room, I threw it in the fire, then went outside and lost my lunch in the bushes." She paused again, but it was as if now that she had started, she couldn't stop. "I don't know how people can do that. I mean, honestly. It's disgusting. Blech. So gross." She shuddered. Leo could hardly feel it because he shook with laughter.

"Oh, Esther. Believe me, someday you won't find it gross."

"That's what my mom said. For the record, I didn't believe her, either."

He was still laughing, but he couldn't help it. She was so clueless. It was adorable.

"I'm serious, Leo. You know me. I'm defunct. I won't like it."

He sobered. "You are not defunct. You are innocent and inexperienced. You need to be guided, to be taught." He frowned again, wondering what man she would find who would be patient, who would understand exactly how innocent and inexperienced she was. Someone who would take his time and be gentle, who wouldn't bumble her into a painful or traumatizing situation.

They lay in heavy silence a while longer. "I read books about kissing," she blurted after a time.

"Because you enjoy kissing?" he asked.

"No," she said, tone impassioned. "Gross. You know how I feel about germs. Disgusting, mouths and tongues. It's a handy way to pass the plague."

Leo couldn't speak for a minute, he was too busy clutching his stomach and laughing. He pressed his palms to his eyes to dry them. "Why did you get books about kissing if you hate it?"

She sighed. "My family was pretty insistent on me marrying Ruben. I figured he had the other part of it down, men usually do. But from what I've observed, women like kissing more than men. So I thought I should probably do some research, bring something to the table."

"And how did it go?" he asked.

She sat up and peered down at him again, face crumpled in disgust. "You think I kissed Ruben? Gross, no way. I was only going to if we had to get married." She tossed herself onto her back again. "Now I'm safe from that. Ick. No way, no how. Not happening."

"What did the books say?" Leo asked. This might be the most fun he'd ever had with a woman, and that said something because he *did* like kissing and everything else that went with it.

"It said you should try to say the names of fruits and vegetables while you kiss. I was with them when it was PEACH and gave them a pass on PLUM, but they lost me at ALFALFA."

Leo was done. If it were possible to die from laughing, he might do it. He was hunched in pain, howling, tears streaking his face. "Oh, Esther. Seriously." She was quiet, but when he caught sight of her face in the moonlight, she smiled.

"You should always laugh, Leo. It lights you up."

He dabbed his eyes and drew a deep breath. "Tell you what, someday I will help you practice kissing, and I promise you will not find it gross."

"Why someday? Why not now?" she asked.

He let out a breath, a shaky one this time and sat up, propping himself on his good side. "Because, Esther, men are not biologically programmed to kiss a woman in a darkened room in bed and then roll over and go quietly to sleep."

"What…oh…*oh.*" She pressed her hands to her cheeks. He couldn't see her, but he knew she blushed.

Smiling, he lay down on his side, resting his head on his arm.

"But you don't like me that way. You wouldn't want to do that with me," she insisted.

"Says you, Esther," he replied.

She was quiet a few beats then, "Gross, Leo. So gross."

Leo lost it again, snorting a laugh as he pressed his face to her shoulder. She rolled away from him. He wondered if she was angry or embarrassed, but she backed against him, nestling. He rested his arm over her waist and leaned up to kiss her cheek.

"Night, Esther."

"Night, Leo."

They were quiet a few minutes and she spoke again. "Is alfalfa really a thing? Does kissing sometimes last that long?"

"Sometimes it's an entire wheat field," he said.

Another pause, then, "I'm going to need a bigger book."

That night marked the first time Leo ever fell asleep laughing.

CHAPTER 18

A few hundred miles away, Cameron Ridge sat staring at his desk, trying to make his mind focus. He never had any trouble whatsoever focusing before Maggie Eldridge came along. Now his mind was a riot of worry and fear. Of course back then he'd also been rudderless and miserably alone, but still. Totally focused. And now all he could see was Maggie's sweet face when he walked in that restaurant and realized she'd been forced to kill someone.

"How is she?"

A minute before, Ridge was alone in the office, and then suddenly The Colonel was there, like mist. If Ridge didn't know better, he might believe The Colonel had the ability to apparate, like a character in a Harry Potter novel. Ridge's door had a distinctive squeak when opened. It was closed before The Colonel's arrival, and closed again after. How did he open it without squeaking? The first time The Colonel made such an appearance in Ridge's life, long ago when he was a SEAL, Ridge predictably flinched. The Colonel had looked at him like he was the worst sort of coward and Ridge swore he would never flinch again. Now, for instance, he merely took a breath and replied as if they were in the middle of a conversation and Ridge hadn't been in the room alone thirty seconds ago.

"She's hanging in there. The call from Bailey helped." Ridge had tried to tell Maggie about his first kill, but it made everything worse. Apparently wives didn't like to hear the thing they had in common with their husbands was taking a person's life. But then their sister-in-law, Bailey, a former Marine Major and The Colonel's daughter, called with sympathetic understanding, and some of the weight seemed to slip off Maggie's shoulders. "She'll be fine, eventually."

"Of course she will. She's a fighter, our Maggie." He shifted and flexed. "And Leo?"

"Still in the wind, or so he believes," Ridge said. Knowing Leo and his suspicions about a mole on the team, Ridge knew he would rabbit. And he knew he wouldn't think to check Esther for a trace, so that's where he'd placed it, on the one thing guaranteed to always be by his side.

"Are they still in the place?" The Colonel asked.

Ridge gave him a nod. His office had been swept for bugs, but still. Couldn't be too careful.

"Are we sure the boy's not the cause of all this?"

Leo and Ridge were nearly the same age, but The Colonel still referred to them as boys. To him, Ridge supposed they were. "I'd stake my life on it," Ridge said. "Leo's a lot of things, traitor's not one of them."

"He's been nearing burnout. Prime pickings for an enemy target," The Colonel said.

"There's exhaustion burnout and then there's anger burnout. Leo's tired, but he's not angry, at least not at us. And, since Esther, he's seemed to revive a bit. I've seen him with her, sir. He's fiercely protective, would die before he'd let anything happen to her."

"How good is he if he's injured?" The Colonel asked.

"Leo's a scrapper, he'll be okay. And for the moment, they're in the safest possible place."

"That leads us back to your team," The Colonel said, which was probably the true reason for his visit.

There was something Ridge needed to say, but it wasn't easy. He took a breath and made himself blurt. "I might be too vested here. I don't know if I can get a clear read on my team." Half the team was his family, for goodness sake. His wife, his brother-in-law. Babs was on the road to being his sister-in-law. LuAnn, Ellen, Blue, they all felt like family, even if they weren't. Ridge hadn't seen this coming. His SEAL team had felt like his brothers; it never occurred to him an office full of civilians could, too.

"We're old school military, not comfortable with mush. But it's not so bad to have feelings, or so my wife tells me."

"My wife tells me the same, but I don't want my judgment compromised by those feelings. I don't want to miss something because I willfully refuse to see it."

"So don't," The Colonel said. "You're the dad of this team, Lieutenant. Dads can love their kids, even when they need discipline. Take a breath, you're on track here."

Ridge took a breath, then another. And he felt better, clearer. Maybe it was the man's faith in him. If The Colonel believed he could do this, he could do this.

"We need to bring Blue in. If we're combing personnel, we'll need him," The Colonel said.

What Ridge needed to say next was similarly uncomfortable, but neither of them had gotten where they were by pussyfooting around feelings. "I'm not sure if I can trust him, not sure if he's clean. There's been a little resentment over Esther. He feels like she's trumped his precious computers and software."

"Has she?" The Colonel asked.

"Multiple times," Ridge said, smirking. Blue was one of the best hackers in the business, and a good guy to boot. Ridge liked him, but it was more than a little amusing to see him taken down a few pegs, to view his flabbergasted reaction when Esther outperformed his software. "As much as I balked about this arrangement, Esther's been an asset, and we're lucky to have her. Her involvement has likely saved hundreds of lives, maybe thousands."

"And also cost someone a whole lot of money," The Colonel interjected. "Girl's a walking target, and soft as mashed potatoes." He swiped a hand over his face. "Blasted politicians, putting civilians in harms way." He took a breath and dropped his hand. "Blue's clean. Bring him in."

Ridge's brows rose. "You put one of your men on him?"

"The boy's marrying my daughter. I put myself on him. If he was dirty, I wanted to know. Believe me, he's clean. His biggest sin is drinking milk straight from the container." He grimaced in a way that made Ridge wonder if he'd personally witnessed such an act. Suddenly he had the vision of Blue standing in his kitchen guzzling milk, The Colonel in the shadows a foot away, undetected. The man was a ghost, could get anywhere unnoticed, soundless and unseen. Ridge was good; Ethan was better; The Colonel was supernatural. Had he ever spied on Ridge that way? Slid into the shadows of his house and observed in order to make sure Ridge was trustworthy? Ridge fought a shudder, thankful once again the man was on his side.

"We're going to have to dismantle everyone, delve into everything, pull it apart, piece by piece," Ridge said. "And we're going to have to do it quickly, before whoever is after Esther finds her." And his wife was going to have a baby, any minute.

"Then let's get to it," The Colonel said, in his steady, reassuring way.

It had the same effect on Ridge as always, a call to action and service, as if his boss knew how to tap into the secret reserves inside him. Ridge sat up, nodded, and pushed away everything but the job. If there was a mole on his team, he was about to find it.

CHAPTER 19

"We need to get back to work," Leo said. He and Esther sat on the floor in front of the sputtering morning fire, huddled together for warmth, eating a breakfast of bread, jam, and coffee.

"I'll pack," Esther said.

"I meant that figuratively. We're going to stay here, but we're going to figure out who wants you dead and why."

"How are we going to do that?" she asked.

"Your brain. We're going to go back through every case you've worked since you started, look for patterns, connections, overlap. I'm sure now you were being followed. There has to be a connection somewhere we've overlooked."

"Okay, Leo," Esther said.

He sighed. "You shouldn't listen to everything I say. Someday I'm going to lie to you."

"I'll know when you're lying," she said.

"No you won't."

"Of course I will."

He sighed again.

"You do that a lot," she noted.

"You stress me," he said, feeling as relaxed as he'd ever felt. It was hard to feel tense about anything in front of a warm fire. And the house itself was so cozy, so clean. Leo had forgotten what it was like to have clean sheets on the bed and a meal on the table, if he'd ever known. Was this what it was like to have a home, a real home with a family who took care of each other?

"*Fȳrgebræc*," Esther said. "The distinct crackling sound of a roaring fire."

"Indeed," Leo agreed.

Esther laughed, smiling up at him. "You don't say indeed."

"Country Leo says indeed now," he replied.

Her hand reached up to smooth his temple. "You seem so relaxed here."

"I am," he agreed. Maybe he would be this way all the time if he lived in the country.

"Was this what you were like as a little boy, before you became a soldier?" she asked.

"No, I was a mean, hard little cuss," he said.

"I find that hard to believe. You were probably sweet and adorable and caring and only pretended to be tough," she said.

"Maybe," he agreed. Back then, he had only pretended to be as hard as he now was.

"I wish we had known each other then," she said.

"You think we would have been friends?" he asked.

She nodded. "Best friends, but only in secret because you would have had to keep pretending to be tough. So we would have had a secret meeting place, a tree house just for you and me. We would meet there at night and I would tell you all the things I learned that day by reading, and you would tell me all the funny things that happened at school. And I would fill it with my words."

He took her coffee, drained it, and set the mug away before pulling her closer, cradling her in his embrace. "What words?" he asked softly. He was already soothed, imagining how it might have been. How would his life have been different if he'd had a friend like Esther when he was a boy and in need of her most?

"Words like *ceraunophilia*, the love of thunder and lightning, *werifesteria*, to wander through a forest in search of mystery. And then I would speak words about you."

"What words about me?" He shifted, resting his head on her stomach while her fingers sifted his hair.

"I would hold you like this and say, 'You're so important, Leo. You're so worthwhile, so kind, so *good*. You're the best part of my world, the favorite part of my day. You matter, you make a difference.'"

He pressed his face to her stomach, hiding the sudden moisture in his eyes. Being with Esther was a healing sort of pain, like lancing an infected wound. Her words scraped the infection away, one painful layer at a time. She hugged him, rubbed the uninjured portion of his back, kissed the top of his head. Leo lay there, wrung out and exhausted, feeling as if he'd run a marathon. Who knew emotional recovery could take such a physical toll?

They lay in perfect silence a long time until he rallied the energy to speak again. "And what would I do for you, in our perfect world?"

"What you already do, bridge the gap to normalcy and fight all the bad guys."

"How is that different from everyone else in your life?" he asked. She had a protective father, brothers, cousins. What made him unique? It was embarrassing how much he wanted to be different from the others.

"To be honest, when we started the job, I thought you would take over. You were the spy, and I was some weird girl. That first day, the phone rang and you picked it up. I thought, *this is it. Another man about to tell me what to do.* But you handed me the phone and let me do my job. Without argument, you've been content to stand back and let me work."

"You're so good at it," he said.

"And you're good at what you do. And that's what makes the difference. No one has ever let me try before. My father, I know he loves me, but he doesn't think I have it in me to succeed. He let me go to college because he didn't know what else to do with me. My sisters married as soon as they turned eighteen, but I had no interest. When I told him I wanted a job, he said I could work at a store for a while until I had babies. If I hadn't won that contest, I'd probably be married to Ruben by now, probably pregnant, definitely miserable."

"How could they have made you marry a man you don't love, why would they?"

"Because they believe it's what's best, because it's the way it's always been, and because…because they believe I'm broken and don't know better."

"Because you're autistic?" he guessed.

She flinched and nodded, swallowing hard. "I didn't know you knew."

"You know I don't care."

"You're the only one. I wasn't diagnosed until I was fifteen. My parents hated the label, thought it made me defunct. To me it was a relief. Finally, a reason I was different. Before that everyone said I was crazy." She tapped her temple. "Why doesn't she talk? Why doesn't she cry or laugh? Why does she count everything, memorize everything? The job at the agency is the first time anyone has ever appreciated my computer brain. Except maybe Blue." They shared a smile. He reached up to caress her face.

"I don't know what's going to happen when this is over, but promise me you won't let anyone make you marry Ruben. You have a sweet, soft heart, too good and too big to be wasted on a bully who can't see it."

"Ruben won't ever marry me now," she said cheerfully. "Divorced women are worth less than autistic ones."

"Hallelujah," he said, and she laughed.

"His face when he thought someone he believed was a liability was wanted by someone like you," she said.

"He should have been more shocked you would want someone like me. Proof his hamster died and the wheel has stopped turning. Although I guess his haircut was all the proof we needed."

She giggled and pressed her face to his good shoulder. "Leo, you're so funny."

He tipped her face and kissed her eyelids and the tip of her nose. She stared at him, unblinking and owlish. "Was that kissing?"

"No, you're not ready for kissing. That's part of the buildup to kissing."

"Why is there a buildup to kissing?" she asked.

"Because sometimes anticipation is the best part," he said.

"That wasn't in any of the books I read," she said.

"We're going off script," he replied.

"I'm not good at winging it," she said.

"That's why you have me. It's my specialty," he said.

She gave a contented little sigh and nestled closer. "I should get dressed. This is the longest I've ever been in my nightgown, I think."

"It's seven in the morning," he said.

"I know. So decadent."

"Stick with me, kid, and I'll have you sleeping 'til noon."

"Is this what you do when we're apart? On our days off?" she asked.

"No, I..." what did he do? His weekends always seemed to pass somehow and then it was Monday again and he was unable to account for the days between. One thing he knew for certain, they were not relaxing. His body felt like his fight-or-flight mechanism had been stuck in the on position since birth. This was the first time he could ever remember feeling calm and relaxed, safe and at peace.

"Maybe I don't ever want to go back," he blurted.

"Then don't," she said simply.

"But what about our job?" he asked.

"It was always going to be temporary. You're my transition guy. What you do next is your decision. What do you want to do next?"

"I have no idea. But I like this feeling. I like not sneaking, lying, shooting, fighting, tailing. It's kind of fun not being a spy for once."

"I know what you want," Esther said.

"What do I want?" he asked, half jokingly, half hopefully.

"You want the same thing I want. You want normal."

He frowned, not for him, but for her. "You're so much better than normal, Esther. You're extraordinary." He tapped her genius brain, able to do what so many others couldn't, to see patterns, details no one else could.

"Back at you, Leo." When she nestled closer, pressing her nose into its spot, he could almost believe her. But the feeling was gone before it could take root.

CHAPTER 20

"We need to begin at the beginning, I think," Esther said. She sat at the scarred wooden table, the piece of paper and pen in front of her now absorbing her total focus. It was her work pose. Her brain had already started clicking through its mental files, arranging them, Leo knew, back to the beginning, their first day of work. In a moment, she would pick up the pen and start to write, likely not stopping until he plucked the pen from her grasp and made her.

Likewise in work mode, Leo was absorbed by watching her. And as usual she had no idea. He stared at her all day every day, wondering what went on in her brain, what made her tick, where she came from, what she did in her off hours. Now he'd filled in some of those gaps. Esther was Amish, she came from an even more conservative, sheltered background than he'd imagined. In her off hours, she was alone. Unlike him, she likely didn't want to be. He had taken what was essentially a fledgling and left her to fend for herself because he didn't want the messiness of being emotionally involved. Too late now, he was up to his eyeballs in emotion, had slept with her in his grasp two straight nights, had cried and been soothed by her. How did he get here?

The one glaring difference from their job, besides the fact that they were in a small house with no electricity, lit only by the sunshine streaming through the windows, was Esther's appearance. Leo was used to the braid and gawky jumpers. Today she'd attempted the messy bun, with very limited success. A large wisp of hair had escaped to torment her, tickling her cheek. It was the sort of touch that drove her crazy, and likely the source of her repeated frowning as she brushed it away and rubbed her cheek. Unbidden, Leo gathered her mass of hair and attempted to rearrange it so it didn't bother her. So complete was her focus, she didn't notice.

Feeling rotten and restless, Leo suddenly wondered how much it would take to break her focus. What would he have to do to get her attention?

He reached for her hand, brushing a kiss over her knuckles. Esther's gaze remained fastidiously on the paper.

He opened her hand and kissed her palm.

Nothing.

He kissed the tip of each finger.

A fleeting glance from the paper to his face and back again. Hmm. She wore one of the new sweaters from the thrift store today. This one had a wide neck that kept sliding off her shoulder. It was likely the most skin she'd ever shown. Leo stared at her shoulder contemplating that fact. The last date he had wore a dress so skimpy it left absolutely nothing to the imagination. Why was the sight of three inches of Esther's shoulder so much more intriguing? Six months ago Leo would have said he didn't do complex. He liked everything simple, straightforward, easy. He was a spy, the end. He liked cheap drinks and even cheaper women, forever and ever, amen. And now he sat in a lightless cabin in the middle of Amish country considering a voluntary end to his career, staring at a woman who thought kissing was a tool of the devil.

He swiped a weary hand over his face, repressed a chuckle, then reached out to tug Esther's sweater back over her shoulder. Like her hair, the sliding sensation was driving her crazy but she was too focused to do anything about it. He meant to tug the sleeve back into place and move away. Instead he slid his hand onto her neck and used it as an anchor, pulling himself closer until his lips were pressed to her throat.

"Leo."

He closed his eyes and inhaled before letting her go and moving away. "What?"

She regarded him with her computer eyes, full of curiosity and confusion, trying to assign a name, category, and meaning to his odd behavior. "What are you doing?"

"Sniffing you."

"Why?"

"Because the smell of you drives me insane with wanting."

"Hmm." She stood, bypassed him, and returned a minute later with something in hand. She set a small glass bottle of Haitian vanilla in front of him and picked up her pen. Leo opened the bottle and sniffed it. It smelled good, but not as good as it smelled on Esther. Somehow the combination of vanilla and Esther's natural essence was more potent than anything he'd ever encountered. Their working days together in the tiny cubicle had become a paroxysm of torture because Leo wasn't joking; the smell made him crazy. He tipped a drop of vanilla on his finger, rubbed it on his own skin and sniffed, grimacing. Not the same, not the same at all. He smelled like burnt cookies. Esther smelled like...well, she smelled like home. He set the bottle away with a sigh, his glance falling on Esther again. She was writing now, meaning she was lost to him until she either finished or he forced her to be done.

"Switch sides with me," she said, startling him. She almost never spoke while she worked.

"Why?"

"You're on the wrong side."

At work she was on his left side, today she was on his right. It wasn't the sort of thing Leo noticed, but of course Esther did; she noticed everything.

"Am I breaking your concentration?" he asked hopefully.

"I need everything to be the same, or a close approximation," she said. She stood, hovering over her chair, waiting for Leo to rise so they could trade places. He pulled her into his lap and wrapped his arms tightly around her.

"How about this?"

"This is not the same," she said, perplexed.

"Maybe it's better," he suggested, giving her a squeeze with his good arm.

She shook her head. With a sigh, he slid into her chair and set her onto his. She picked up her pen, held it aloft, and set it down again. Then she slid into his lap and hugged his neck, being careful to avoid his injury.

"It is better, but not for work. I like touching you, Leo. Only you, because you're special to me. You're my favorite." She pressed her palms to his cheeks and smiled.

She was so sweet, so pure. Leo felt the familiar sense of panic and appreciation that he was now her person, but something new was mixed in, something he wasn't yet ready to examine or name. Esther rested her head on his shoulder. His hand smoothed up and down her spine, and he kissed the top of her head. A deep peace washed over him, like someone upended a bottle of peace oil and poured it over his head, anointing him with it. This was what he had needed for years, a chance to get away from it all, to think, to address all the issues he hadn't wanted to. He was going to have to find a way to revisit this feeling later, after everything was over. His mind envisioned the little cabin, the dream one he'd been building in his head. It began to feel tangible, as if he might actually be able to go there. Maybe he could hire Esther's uncle to build it for him. He had certainly done a spectacular job with his own house and the *Dawdy haus* they currently inhabited.

Esther was calm and quiet, her hand pressed to his chest, but he wasn't fooled by her silence.

"You're thinking about work, aren't you?" he asked.

"Yes," she said. It would never occur to her to lie to him. Her frankness was both a blessing and a curse. If he screwed up, she would be the first to let him know, in no uncertain terms. On the other hand, Leo had spent so much of his life lying, running, hiding, playing games, it was a wonderful anomaly to be with someone who did none of those things.

"Okay, back to it," he said, sliding her off his lap once again and depositing her in the chair.

She picked up the pen but didn't yet put it to paper. Instead she faced him. "I'm sorry. It's how my brain works."

"Don't be sorry. I love how your brain works." It was true, he did. However much Esther might view it as a curse that she was atypical, Leo saw it as a gift. No one could do what she did. Lucky him she was his...work assignment. What had initially seemed like a loser job, protecting someone no one wanted, had turned out to be the best thing that ever happened to him. And how ironic that he'd not only been shot protecting her, but she was now so valuable she was wanted by someone powerful and dangerous enough to hire a mercenary to take her out.

Remembering anew how much danger she was in also turned his focus back to work. He tapped the paper in front of her. "Get started. The answer is in your mind somewhere. Let's find it."

With a slight nod of agreement, Esther faced forward and started to write.

CHAPTER 21

"It's weird to be here without her."

Cameron Ridge looked at Blue over the desk between them. "I know."

"It's weird to be in your office working, just the two of us," Blue continued. Ridge's office was the only place of guaranteed safety until they could determine whether or not they had a mole.

"Yep."

"It's weird…"

Cam set down his pen with a sigh and looked up. "You're purposely trying to provoke me by making idle small talk, huh?"

"Yup."

"Quit it."

"Okay." Blue put his head down and resumed typing. Unlike Esther, he was not one of those people who needed total concentration on his work to be effective. In fact, his brain seemed to enjoy having a distraction. Locked in Ridge's office, he was void of handy distractions, minus his sometimes-surly boss. Since Maggie started her maternity leave, he was more surly than sometimes. He clicked his pen a few times until Ridge made a not-so-subtle motion toward his gun. Blowing out a breath, Blue tossed his pen aside. "How's she doing?"

The "she" in question was always Maggie, the strongest source of any connection between them. Without her, they would likely not be friends. They certainly had little in common—geeky hacker and suave SEAL turned spy. Except Ridge's brother was married to Blue's fiancée's sister, so they were almost sort of family, if you tilted your head and squinted really hard. But it wasn't the in-law connection that bridged them; it was Maggie, Ridge's wife and one of Blue's closest friends. She was like a little sister to him, and he felt protective of her. He hated that she'd had to kill someone at such a critical time when she should be feeling nothing but ecstatic excitement over the baby.

"How is she?" Blue repeated when he couldn't take the ten second stretch of silence any longer. Couldn't they bring Babs in on this? He and Babs were close the way he and Maggie were close, and she dated Maggie's brother. No way she was the mole. Although Babs had been sort of dreamy and distracted ever since the shooting. He wondered if she was equally traumatized by seeing a man get killed. She was soft like that, like Maggie.

"She's fine," Ridge said distractedly.

"Really?" Blue asked. Ridge didn't like to talk about feelings or personal stuff at work. Or outside of work. That privilege was reserved for Maggie, unlike Blue who wore his thoughts and feelings on his sleeves, literally with tattoos.

"Really, really."

"Were you purposely quoting *Shrek* just then?" Blue asked.

Ridge looked up long enough to give him the death glare before dropping his head again.

"It's not just that Maggie's soft," Blue continued as if they were in a back and forth conversation and his words weren't pinging off Ridge like spitballs. "It's that she's so innocent and untouched."

Realizing he wasn't going to be able to blow off the conversation or ignore Blue like he wanted, Ridge set down his pen and rubbed the bridge of his nose. "Maggie is soft and sweet, but she is also steely and determined. She has a lot of rational sense, and she knows she did the right thing. That knowledge is helping her cope with what is obviously a difficult situation, but she'll be fine."

Blue blinked at him a minute and grinned. "You bugged her about how she was doing until she said those words and now you're direct quoting her, huh?"

Ridge resumed staring at his paper. "Shut up, Blue." His cheeks were slightly pink, telling Blue his guess was correct.

"It's probably true, though. Maggie has hidden depths of rage and protectiveness. Wouldn't want to get caught between her and Amelia when they're angry." He shuddered.

"No, you wouldn't," Ridge said mildly.

Blue tipped his head, studying him. "What's the worst fight you and Maggie ever had?"

"Even if I weren't your boss, do you think I would tell you that?" Ridge returned without glancing up.

"I like to know things about people," Blue admitted the obvious truth. "Hidden things they'd rather keep secret. Gives me a creepy sort of thrill."

"Jane's a lucky, lucky woman," Ridge muttered.

"Oh, come on. When you were in the field, you can't tell me you didn't get a little high off digging deep and finding hidden information. If not, what's the point?"

"Uh, protecting national security?" Ridge said.

"All I'm saying is, it's fun to spy on people. I'm just honest enough to admit it," Blue said.

Ridge gave him a wry smile. "Do you think it's fun to be spied on?"

Blue shrugged. "Who cares? We're the top of the top, the best of the best. No one's going to spy on us."

Ridge envisioned Blue guzzling milk from the jug, The Colonel on standby, watching in secret. Only this time the memory was hilarious and he laughed.

"One day without your wife here to stand guard, and your brain broke," Blue said.

"Don't you have work to do? And, believe it or not, I'm asking not only as someone who is annoyed by your inane chatter, but also as, wait for it, your *boss*." He dropped his pen as if he were dropping a mic.

"I'm getting shades of what you were like before Maggie entered the picture and made you likeable. Not going to lie, don't care for you as much without her," Blue said.

"Me neither," Ridge said unconcernedly, reaching for his pen again.

"For your information, I am working. I'm waiting—oh so patiently —for the decryption on the stuff I took from everyone's phones this morning." A little ping went off beside his head and he scooted back to stare at his screen. "Huh."

"What?" Ridge asked, sitting up straighter. He knew his team pretty well by now. Despite how much he and Blue liked to poke at each other, they were friends who had spent a lot of time together, both in and out of work. He knew when Blue was serious, knew when he was concerned. He had that look now.

Blue cleared his throat and swiped a hand over his neck. "It's, uh, something from Babs's phone."

Ridge tensed. *Not Babs.* Maggie would be crushed. He forced himself to take a deep breath and push away his emotion. "What is it? And don't hold back or I'll literally break one of your bones, starting with your toes so you'll still be able to type."

Blue took a deep breath and said it in a rush. "Secret meetings, looks like a rendezvous. Something she's obviously trying to keep hidden."

"With who?"

Blue shrugged. "Don't know who the other end is. Looks like a burner phone."

Ridge pressed his palms into the table. Not good, not good at all. "Let's bring her in." He reached for his phone and dialed Babs's number, hoping against hope he wasn't about to arrest his employee, his wife's friend, his brother-in-law's girlfriend.

CHAPTER 22

They were working in order, starting from the first day they arrived at the new job. "Blue called and sent me the email with those pictures," Esther remembered, gazing into the middle distance.

"And then you smoked him and his stupid computer by proving his software messed up."

Unlike him, she didn't look pleased by the memory. "I'm pretty sure he hates me."

"So what?"

"So it's not actually fun to be disliked, especially not by someone everyone in the office adores," she said. "That's why I..."

She broke off, staring into space, lips pressed together.

"Why you what?" Leo pressed.

"Took a dive on chess."

Leo had to think a second to remember. Maggie and Babs had been taunting Blue, saying Esther was like Gary Kasparov who beat the IBM computer, Deep Blue, at chess. They called him Deep Blue the entire morning. Blue had tried to laugh it off, but everyone could tell he was irritated by the thought of Esther beating his software. So he challenged her to a chess match against his computer. The computer won, and Blue had been triumphant. Leo hadn't thought anything of it, because who beats a computer? Esther, apparently, if she let herself.

"Don't do that," he said now. "Don't try to make yourself less so others will accept you. If Blue doesn't like you, that's his problem. Besides, I don't think he dislikes you; I think he's intimidated by you. Before you arrived, he was the golden boy, the most necessary member of the team. Enter Esther, who found the things he and his precious computer missed."

"I wasn't trying to show him up or make him feel bad," she said.

"I know but, Es, you can't control how other people feel. You can only control what you do, and you've done nothing wrong."

"I know I'm doing a good job, Leo. My work is solid, but…" She pressed her lips together and looked away again.

"But what?" he asked, his tone laden with preemptive sympathy because he already knew.

"I want them to like me. I want to be friends, a part of the team."

"We're a team," he reminded her.

She nodded, eyes downcast.

"Hey," he said, tipping her face to his. Her eyes were watery, and he couldn't take it. She was so sweet and loving and kind. How could everyone else not see that? "I like you." His hands slid to her cheeks, his thumb easing over her bottom lip.

"Are you going to kiss me?" she whispered.

"Do you want me to?" he returned.

"I'm torn between curiosity and revulsion."

He snorted a laugh, and she continued. "Also, I know you said building anticipation is supposed to make me like kissing, but it's making me anxious, like you're going to spring from behind a hidden bush and take control of my lips or something."

He laughed harder and used one of his hands to dab his eyes. "There's an easy way to solve that."

"There is? What?"

"You could kiss me," he said.

"What would be the point of that? You're kissing me so you can teach me, but you already know how to kiss. You don't need me to do it."

"Why has it never occurred to you that I might want you to do it? That I volunteered to teach you because I think about kissing you every moment of every day we're together?"

She blinked at him. "But you don't kiss girls like me."

"What kind of girls do you think I kiss?"

"Normal girls."

He shook his head. "I kiss women who are broken, like me. Maybe I want to kiss someone whole, someone who isn't playing a game or trying to take something from me. Maybe I want to kiss someone who will be thinking of all the ways she wants to take care of me."

"I would be thinking that," Esther admitted.

"I know, because it's what you do. You take care of me in all the ways."

"You took a bullet for me, so it would seem that it's reciprocal," Esther said.

"I'm certain you are the only woman who could say reciprocal and make me want to kiss you more," he said.

"What if it's gross and I want to push you away?" she asked.

"Then push me away," he said. "I won't be upset, I promise. A first kiss is a big deal, it might take a few practice tries to get it right, for you to become comfortable."

"I'm always comfortable with you, Leo." She stood on her toes and brushed her lips gently to his, almost as if she were shaking her head no while involving their lips. Leo was so shocked that she made the first move he remained staring at her, wide eyed and frozen.

"Was that not how it's done? Did I mess it up already?" she asked.

He had to clear his throat before he could get words out. "That was the opposite of wrong. That was kind of a next level pro move."

"Big fat sarcasm?" she guessed, eyes wide with worry.

He shook his head and brushed his lips on hers. She clutched his shirt harder and leaned into him, all enthusiasm now. He cupped her face again, slowing her pace, kissing her slowly and gently, instructing her without making it obvious he was doing so. As with everything, Esther was a quick and brilliant student. She followed his lead and matched him, whisper-soft kiss to whisper-soft kiss. If he'd ever kissed a girl this way—so gently and tenderly—he couldn't remember. Suddenly he wondered why not. It was far, far more intense than some previous face-swallowing sessions he'd indulged in. Why was he always in such a mad rush to get to the next level? Why didn't he ever pause to consider the beauty in staying put? Esther could not be rushed, she was far too innocent and inexperienced for that. Leo thought he would hate having to instruct a woman in this way. Instead he felt almost giddy with the power of it. She was moldable, a complete novice, and he desperately wanted to mold her in the way that would be most beneficial to her. One step at a time, gently, carefully.

That was why, after a few innocent kisses, he backed away and put space between them, to check on her, to assess the damage and make certain she was okay.

She opened her eyes and pressed her fingers to her flushed cheeks. "I can now say with absolute certainty that revulsion is no longer part of the conversation." She took a step toward him, hand reaching for his face, but Leo took a step back and captured her hand in his instead.

"Let's put a stopper in that bottle for now because…" he couldn't begin to tell her why. How could he possibly explain how easily and how quickly one thing led to another to a grown woman who was as inexperienced as a preschooler? "Because your pretty lips would get chapped, and nobody wants that kind of pain."

Esther nodded seriously, buying his excuse completely. Or so he thought. "Also my mom said sex starts with kissing, and I know I'm not ready for that."

Leo choked on air and coughed for a solid twenty seconds, nodding a few times before he could speak. "Right, there's also that."

"Are you okay?" she asked.

He pulled her close and hugged her, wrapping her tight with his good arm. "Your complete lack of filter might be my undoing one day."

"Big fat sarcasm?" she asked, confused.

"Maybe, not sure that time." He kissed the top of her head and a minute later they returned to work.

CHAPTER 23

"*Y*ou *eloped?*"

It was the fourth time Ridge said it, but the shock hadn't begun to wear off. After hauling a nervous-looking Babs into his office and explaining their suspicions over the burner phone, she quickly blurted an explanation. Somehow Ridge would have been less surprised if she had turned out to be the mole.

"You're telling me you eloped with Darren Eldridge, my brother-in-law, the man who, at my wedding, commented how modern and non-traditional we were because I didn't wear tails and a top hat? That Darren? He eloped on a whim?"

Beside them, Blue laughed hysterically, as he had been since Babs's big announcement. Then he sobered and sat up. "Wait a minute. This means everyone in the office got married before Jane and me. She is going to *kill* me."

Babs tossed him an annoyed look. "So set a date already."

"We were waiting until all the babies were born so Bailey and Poppy could be there and, you know, Comic Con is coming up and..." he trailed off and wiped a bead of perspiration from his forehead and shoved Babs hard in the shoulder. "She's seriously going to kill me. Thanks for ruining my life."

"It's not Babs's fault you're dragging your feet to the altar, Grandpa," Ridge said. "Though it is her fault she *eloped without telling anyone.*"

Babs put her hands to her head. "I know, I *know.* It was the night of the shooting. Darren drove me home and we parked and then he sat there, staring into space. I touched his arm and asked if he was okay, and he got out, opened my door, got down on two knees, not just one, and said he adored me and McKenna and life was short and would I marry him. Of course I said yes. I thought we would set a date, plan an event, but he got back in the car and drove to the airport where we flew to Vegas. You know how Darren is when he gets something in his head, there's really no changing it."

"The Eldridge curse," Ridge said, hand pressed over his eyes.

"Maggie and Amelia are going to kill me, aren't they?" Babs asked. She sounded miserable.

"Are you joking? They're going to be ecstatic," Ridge said, dropping his hand. "Their parents, on the other hand." It was the second time one of their children tied the knot in secret, including Amelia and Ethan who got married in Africa.

Babs blew out a breath, sounding slightly less frantic. "Right, okay, forget it. I'm wearing this now." She reached in her pocket, pulled out a giant rock, and slid it on her finger.

"Holy cow, what do geologists get paid?" Blue asked, snagging her finger and bringing it closer for inspection.

"He didn't buy it; he mined it."

Ridge and Blue blinked at her, uncomprehending. "What?" Ridge said at last.

"He mined it. Dug it out of the earth with his own two hands," Babs said.

"Like a dwarf in Middle Earth?" Blue asked. Babs slugged him in the shoulder and Ridge snickered.

"I think it's romantic," she said, looking slightly diminished so that Ridge and Blue felt immediate guilt.

"So it is. Congratulations. I guess you're officially my sister-in-law now," Ridge said. If he sounded anything less than thrilled it was because this news only added one more layer of complication to an already complicated situation. How was he supposed to be objective when half the people who worked for him were related?

"Congratulations, Babulous," Blue said, hugging her. "You deserve all the happiness in the world, and I'm so glad you found some."

"Thank you," Babs said, sparkling joy restored. And then she sat up straighter as a new thought occurred. "Wait a minute, how did you know? Why did you bring me in here?"

Blue looked to Ridge, uncertain if they were still keeping her in the dark. Ridge blew out a breath. "The night of the shooting, the guy knew where everyone would be, down to where they'd be sitting. And before that, Leo thought Esther was being followed."

"You think there's a mole," Babs said.

Ridge nodded.

"What was the burner phone about?" Blue asked. He didn't sound apologetic. In their line of work, privacy was a myth. The only way to be above suspicion was to be transparent.

"Darren tried to take a selfie of us in front of one of the fountains in Vegas and dropped his phone. He bought a burner until he could get it replaced. I can't believe you think there's a mo…" She gripped the edge of Ridge's desk and sat up straight.

"What is it?" Ridge asked, suddenly alert. Like Blue earlier, he knew Babs well enough by now to know when it was something important.

"I think I might… but no, it's not…but if…" she sputtered.

"Babs, what?" Ridge said in the Dad tone they all responded to immediately.

"After Maggie figured out Esther was autistic, we started making a concerted effort to be nicer to her, to reach out."

"Esther's autistic?" Blue interjected.

"Another time," Ridge snapped. "But yes, where have you been? Maybe take out the earbuds and interact with actual humans occasionally. Resume." He flicked his fingers at Babs.

"Anyway, I started talking to her, trying to get her to warm up, feel more comfortable. It was hard with Leo always hovering protectively nearby, ready to snap our hands off if he thinks we're getting too close and might hurt her. But one day he went out to get their lunch from the car. Esther was in the break room, and we spent some time talking, actually talking. I asked her a lot of questions about herself, where she was from, how she got here, personal things. To my surprise, she answered, seemed glad someone finally asked."

"Babs, the point," Ridge said, making a "hurry up" motion with his hand. He was a cut-to-the-chase type person, not one for embellishments, especially when the life of one of his team might be on the line.

Babs started to sniffle. "Yesterday someone asked me about her, asked me what I knew about her, where I thought she went. I didn't think anything about it because it felt so conversational and because I had no idea you were searching for a mole, but I told what I knew, that Esther was Amish. I said if she and Leo were going to hide, I bet they would go to her Amish family in New York."

Ridge's fingers curled into fists. He had the feeling he was going to hate whatever he heard next. "Who asked the question?" he said slowly, deliberately.

"You're not going to believe it," Babs said, then took a breath and upended their world.

CHAPTER 24

Leo woke in the morning, Esther's hair draped over his face like a sleep mask. Not that the darkness of the room needed any embellishments. The barest hint of dawn peeked through a crack in the curtain, illuminating them in its weak light. He lay perfectly still, letting the renewed peace of the morning wash over him. He couldn't quite wrap his mind around that peace. Usually he woke in a mild panic, disoriented, tense, adrenaline pumping. Years and years of being on assignment, of waking in strange beds, motels, and countries had taught him to never fully trust those first few moments until he became oriented. He had started doing it in his apartment—waking in a sweat, wondering where he was, if he was in danger.

But now, even before he opened his eyes, he knew. Middle of Nowhere, New York. Amish cabin. Esther tucked safely beside him. His heart rate was steady, his breathing normal. No sweating or trembling. Everything was as it should be, and how long had it been since he could say that? Had he ever been able to say that? Even as a kid he'd woken up sick with dread, wondering if his dad would be angry and drunk or, worse, gone, wondering if his mom would cry, wondering if there would be enough food on the table. He thought when he grew up, became a man, and started making his own money and decisions, everything would be fixed.

For a few years in the marines, life was better. They were fully in charge of his destiny, always telling him where to go or what to do. Leo had taken to it like the proverbial duck to water. For a few grasping years, he had felt safe, even in the midst of war. And then The Colonel got hold of him and began to whisper in his ear. *Talent like yours is wasted being a jarhead. Time for you to steer your own course, make your own way. You have the skills we're looking for.*

And so Leo had left the security of the marines for a chance to prove himself as a spy. It had its perks, for certain. He hadn't been under anybody's thumb, per se. The autonomy had been a relief after having so much of his life ordered by the military. But the weight of his past always caught up, both his family life and the incident. Men had died on his watch. Nothing was ever okay after that.

Enter Esther.

As if thinking about her made her wake, she opened her eyes and looked at him with her computer look. She was curious and about to ask him a question. One never knew what it might be. Once in the middle of the day at work she turned to him and asked if he thought black holes were a portal to heaven. He still puzzled over that one.

"Do people kiss in the mor..." she began, but the question was answered before it could be completed when he leaned forward and kissed her.

Last night they hadn't resumed kissing after those first few gentle exchanges. Leo hadn't wanted to push her and, if he was being honest, he hadn't wanted to push himself. Being concerned about a partner's wellbeing was so new he was afraid he would trample it, would collapse under the weight of temptation if he and Esther spent much more time engaged in physical contact. *INNOCENT, INNOCENT, INNOCENT,* his mind screamed at him all the time like a warning beacon. Until this moment when she woke in his embrace looking like spring's first rosebud. Also, he was apparently the type of man who had thoughts about spring's first rosebud now.

Right away this kissing was much more intent than last night's had been, but Esther kept pace. She didn't seem frightened or disgusted. Quite the contrary. One of her hands eased into his hair, her fingers scraping his scalp in her attempt to draw him impossibly closer. One of her legs hitched onto his hip and Leo rolled away from her, gobsmacked.

She sat up and peered down at him, annoyed. "Why did you stop kissing when I've decided once and for all I like it?"

His laughter worked to dispel a bit of the heavy tension, at least on his end. "Because you're killing me."

Now her eyes rounded with worry. She was far too literal. "Not really. Your, uh, leg migrated." He tapped her knee, still pressed to his thigh.

Esther glanced down at it as if it belonged to someone else. "How did that get there?"

He laughed again. "I think biology began to take over," he explained, reaching her hand and winding their fingers together.

"And that's why you stopped? Because that upsets you?"

"Uh, no, far from it. I stopped because biology began to take over for me, too." He pulled her down beside him, safely out of reach of his lips, and kissed the top of her head. She rested her cheek on his chest, pondering.

"There's so much I don't know, Leo. So much."

"You'll get there," he assured her. He brought her hand to his mouth and kissed it. She stared up at him with big eyes, and he froze. He knew her so well he could read the question in her eyes. *With you?* And she knew him so well she could likely read the answer in his. *Don't ask.* For once, she found her internal filter and didn't ask. Leo was both relieved and disappointed by that.

He'd been on assignment before, lots of times, enough to know the score. Things were intense. They'd been through a lot. But forced intimacy wasn't real. He and Esther were friends, yes. Partners, true. But they were far too different for anything more than that. A lasting relationship between them would never work, mostly because Leo would find some way to screw it up. He could feel the panic making a return and worked to push it away. He cared about her far too much to inflict himself on her. Country Leo was an anomaly. If they could stay here, he would be fine. If real life wouldn't intrude, he and Esther could be equals. Back at work, back in the city, he would revert to his normal self: unreliable, unstable, cruel, selfish, broken. Esther's opposite in every way.

"Everything works with you," Esther said, sounding awed. "I don't like to touch people. It's too much sensory overload, but you…" She picked up his hand and smoothed her fingers over his. "I thought I would hate kissing, but no, you make that good, too. You understand the way my brain works and allow it to do its thing. You give me hope, Leo. You make me feel like normal doesn't matter because what we have is better than normal." She kissed his palm, she who hated germs and hated kissing, had crossed the invisible barriers and made a tangible gesture, and what did Leo do in return? Nothing, absolutely nothing. He stared at the ceiling, fighting the panic that once again tried to climb up his throat. Even Esther, who wasn't astute about matters of the heart, would have to notice his silence, his lack of response.

When she threw off the covers and darted out of the room, his heart sank. He would have to go to her, would have to somehow make amends for all he hadn't said, hadn't done, hadn't promised. He would have to tell her the truth—that he was unable to do what she needed him to do in this instance, to be who she needed him to be.

Reluctantly, he pushed off the covers and padded to the kitchen, expecting to see Esther busying herself with the fire or with breakfast. It was her M/O when she was upset to fuss over him, to take care of him, even when she hurt. But the fire was still cold and there was no comforting smell of coffee or oatmeal. Esther sat at the table, pen aloft.

Not angry—working.

"What's up, sweetheart?" *Yes, stupid, throw endearments in there to confuse the situation. Good luck explaining to the ingénue how you kiss her and call her pet names and don't want to be more than friends. Way to keep a cap on it.*

"There's something on the tip of my brain I can't quite retrieve, a connection."

"How can I help?"

"Sit on the other side of me," she said, not bothering to look up. He sat on the side he usually sat on and stared longingly at the empty fireplace. He shivered and ran his hand up and down his arm. Esther's arms also had goose bumps.

"I need to see to the fire," he said. She didn't respond. Maybe she had only needed him to sit in his regular spot to get in the zone. Now that she was in it, it was probably okay for him to move around.

He left her side, started the fire, and attempted to make coffee. Making coffee manually and without electricity was a whole different ballgame. His wasn't as good as hers, but it was hot and caffeinated. He set a mug before Esther who, predictably, ignored it. He picked up her hand and wrapped it around the mug. She brought it to her lips on rote, took a sip, and set it back down again. He was about to tackle breakfast when one of the cousins from the main house knocked on the door and shyly presented some coffee cake and milk.

"Bless you, kid," Leo said and the boy's cheeks flushed crimson. *Adorable,* Leo thought, patting the boy's head before he skittered off. *Did I just pat an Amish kid's head and bless him? Yes, yes I did.* Country Leo might need beaten up soon to get things back in order. A few more days of pastoral life and he might become a pacifist himself. Maybe he'd convert and follow Aaron into carpentry. *Those haircuts, though,* he thought, shaking his head as he closed the door with his foot. Plus he'd never been able to grow a proper beard.

"Esther, should I convert and become Amish?" he said, knowing she would completely ignore him, which she did. He downed a piece of coffee cake, broke off a piece, and stuffed it in Esther's mouth. When she swallowed, he nudged her hand toward the coffee mug again, and she downed that, too. "Like feeding a baby bird," he mused. He sat down beside her, resuming his post as a creepy stalker. She didn't have the kind of flashy features that would catch anyone's attention from across a crowded room, wasn't the sort who would make guys nudge each other when she walked in. But the beauty was there, for anyone patient enough to search for it. Her complexion was flawless, her delicate features perfectly arranged. Leo understood Amelia's fascination with her because with a new hairstyle and some makeup, she could be a knockout. He didn't want her to be a knockout, however, and not because he didn't want other men to look at her, but because he found her perfect as she was. She was so…pure. He hated it when women took off their makeup and looked like a completely different person, but it was something more than that. It was that she never tried to be anything other than what she was. There was no pretense with Esther, and her sweet face and outlandishly long hair were evidence of that.

He rested his head on her shoulder and pressed a kiss to her throat, thoroughly expecting her to continue to ignore him, as was their custom. But she put down her pen and hugged him, clasping his head against her as she smoothed her hand over his hair. She kissed the top of his head. "My sweet Leo."

If his eyes didn't suddenly burn so badly, he would have laughed. In his whole life, no one had ever called him sweet, and certainly not a woman. "I didn't think you noticed me when you worked."

"I always notice you, but I'm finished working."

He sat up and studied her. "You figured it out?"

"I figured it out." She reached for the paper and pulled it closer. "The first day, the pictures Blue sent me. They were the same man, Aleksandr Nabokov, and that's what's been bothering me, because once we realized he was two people, we stopped looking for others."

"I'm not sure I follow." He broke off another piece of cake and stuffed it into her mouth. She chewed and swallowed before she answered.

"He's more than one person. He's a master of changing his appearance. You were right, he was following me."

He blinked at her. "You saw his other disguises? You know he followed you?"

She nodded. "I did what Blue did that day. I went through everyone we've worked, everyone who was on the train that day and overlaid their faces. There were two more matches."

"The guy who wants you dead, the guy who paid someone to have you shot, the terrorist and mass murderer whose alias you busted, this Aleksandr Nabokov, got close enough to be on the train with you?"

"Yes. And he's also been pretending to work at my library."

"Library guy is the one?"

She nodded and reached for more of the cake. "Also, you should definitely not convert and become Amish, Leo. You should be you, exactly as you are because you're the best man I've ever known. And I hope it's not like feeding a baby bird. Gross." She grimaced, likely imagining him regurgitating her food.

He pressed the heel of his hand to his eye socket. "Esther, your range of experience is vastly limited. I am not the best man, I'm not even a good man."

"I didn't say you were the best man in the world; I said you were the best man I've ever known. Though, given your competition is Ruben Miller, it's probably not much of a compliment," she said, breaking off a piece of coffee cake and pushing it in her mouth to hide her smile.

Leo bit her neck, causing her to squeal and back away from him. "Stop teasing, go back to adoring," he pled.

"Okay," she agreed and slid herself into his lap. His hand eased up and down her spine and she sighed tiredly.

"Do you know who the mole is?"

"Not enough data for that," she replied.

Now it was his turn to sigh. "Es, I'm going to have to call Ridge. He's going to make us come in."

"It was always going to happen eventually," she said, but she sounded as sad and resigned as he did.

"I'm not exaggerating when I say these have been the best few days of my life," he said. "And I say that as someone who was recently shot."

"All my days are good with you, Leo."

"Yes, but this was something special."

"Being fake married agrees with us, I think," she said.

He tensed, waiting for her to ask for promises about their future, for reassurances. When she didn't, he felt the same curious mix of annoyance and relief from earlier. "How would your aunt and uncle feel if we borrowed some clothes?"

She peeled back to look at him. "You want to be Amish for a day?"

"I want to blend in. In this town, the English stand out. It's safer if we play the part." He felt antsy and alert, that gut sixth sense feeling that had been absent for days. Whether it was because they could now assign an identity to their assailant or because something was about to happen, he couldn't say. "I wish I had more ammo."

"I'm sure you could borrow one of my uncle's hunting rifles or shotguns," Esther said.

It was better than nothing, but it wasn't as if he could carry one of those on his person. Still, having it on standby would make him feel more secure. "We need to teach you to shoot, Es."

"I can't. I'm a pacifist," she said.

"I thought that was an Amish thing," he said.

"Mennonite, too."

"How can you reconcile being a pacifist with being a spy?" he asked.

She shrugged. "I like to think I'm stopping bad guys with guns from using them in a nonviolent way. Totally pacifist."

"How can you be a pacifist and reconcile being with someone like me?" he asked.

She turned her face to his and gave him a sweet Esther smile of understanding, the kind that added more spackle to all the holes inside him. "My beliefs are my beliefs, Leo, not yours. I would never impose that on you. Each of us has to reconcile within ourselves."

"What if you had to protect someone you care about?" he asked.

"I would try to do it without using violence," she said.

"That's never feasible," he said, feeling frustrated for reasons he didn't understand.

"Okay, Leo," she said, nestling.

He hugged her, feeling like it was the end of everything. This morning he had felt such peace, and now it was all draining away. "Esther, Esther, Esther, what am I going to do with you?"

"I don't think you actually want me to answer that question with a suggestion," she said.

"No, probably not. We should get going."

She started to ease away from him. He pulled her back. "Whatever happens after this, you are… This has been…"

"*Abditory*, a hiding place." She kissed him, an affectionately soft press of lips. "*Lodestone*, something that attracts strongly." She kissed him again. "*Skookum*, excellent, first rate." She kissed him again and pulled back, waiting for him to speak. Leo said the only thing that came to him.

"Wow." He tipped her face and kissed her, and neither of them spoke again for a long time.

CHAPTER 25

"I should be the one to drive the buggy, I think," Leo said. They were clip clopping their way to town, the reins in Esther's hands.

"You don't know how. And you're injured," she reminded him.

"Yes, but all the other Amish men are the ones who drive," he replied.

Esther snickered, and he elbowed her. "Are you making fun of me for comparing myself to the Amish?"

"No, I'm making fun of you because you believe you come up short," she replied, and he sighed.

"You always say the right thing," he said.

"You're the only one who believes that, Leo."

"Isn't that enough?" he asked.

"Yes," she agreed.

The buggy provided some measure of security, oddly enough since they were basically exposed. But it was dark and, if they reclined slightly, they couldn't be seen. Since Leo's phone was dead and there was no way to recharge it, they had to drive to the community telephone attached to a pole at the other end of the village. Leo felt itchy. It was the way he always felt before the action went down. He swallowed hard and tried to push away his anxiety. The hand gripping his gun was sweaty. Three shots, that was how many he had left. Three shots and an injured shoulder and an untrained pacifist in his care. The odds weren't in their favor, but that was assuming they were found. It was highly possible their cover was still intact. Leo had no reason to believe it was blown, other than his newfound anxiety. Then again, they hadn't left the cabin in a few days. Maybe it was merely the exposed feeling of being away from their hideout, their *abditory.*

He scanned each face they passed, searching for a disguise, not that it did much good. Esther was the only one who could ID him, whose computer brain could spot the similarities in facial features well enough to connect the dots. And she had only done it by studying pictures. Could she do it live and in person? And who was to say it would be the same man? Last time he hired a mercenary to take them out. He could do that again. Just because he was a bloodthirsty maniac with the ability to kill them himself didn't mean he would.

A car blurred by them and Leo sat forward for a double take. Was that…? It had looked like… But, no, that was impossible. And if it was, they were in bigger trouble than he realized.

"Did you see that car?" Leo asked.

"No," Esther replied. "I was concentrating on the horses so they didn't spook. They seem pretty solid, but I've only done this once before, a long time ago."

Leo was more than antsy now; he buzzed with adrenaline. Everything in him told him something bad was about to go down. Their cover was blown, they'd been found, Aleksandr was coming for them. And if he just saw who he thought he saw, the mole was someone more lethal than he could handle. He swallowed hard and dabbed at his forehead.

"Es, I need you to be on full alert, okay? Scan everybody and let me know if you see anyone you know from DC. Even if you're not sure, let me know, okay? Stick close and do exactly as I say. If I say down, lie down. If I say run, run like you've never run before, okay?"

"Okay, Leo," she replied. Her calm steadiness did a little to soothe him. He took a deep breath and then another, wiped his gun hand on his leg to clear the sweat. He hadn't been this nervous in…he had

never been this nervous. The stakes were higher than they had ever
been. He was all that stood between Esther and certain doom and he
wasn't enough, had never been enough. She patted his leg. "Sangfroid,
Leo."

At the very least, her words provided a distraction. "What's that
one again?"

"Coolness of mind, calmness, composure. Find yours, please."

"I can't let anything happen to you," he choked.

"That works both ways," she said.

"I'm the one who takes care of you," he said.

"No, we take care of each other. And everything will be okay, one
way or another. Have faith."

"That's the problem, sweetheart. I'm not the one with the faith;
you are."

"Find some. In the meantime, I'll lend you mine." She pulled the
horses to a halt, jumped down, and wrapped the reins around a
hitching post. Since there was only one phone and a large community
of Amish, it was a popular destination. The line to use it looked
massive, at least twenty Amish bundled by groups with more on
the way.

"This is too open, too exposed," Leo muttered, but Esther was
already taking his hand and tugging him toward the line.

They got a lot of looks. The woman in front of them spoke to
Esther in Pennsylvania Dutch. Leo couldn't understand the words, of
course, but he got the gist. *Where are you from, Strangers?* While all
Amish people looked the same to him, they were a tightknit community, easily distinguishable from each other. Esther and the woman
chatted a few moments. Leo recognized Lydia and Aaron's names, so
she must have told them some story about visiting her family. He kept
his back to her, scanning the crowd, his unease growing with every
passing moment.

More people arrived and began clumping together to talk. The
communal phone must be the Amish version of a water cooler.
Instead of one orderly line, there was now a snaking line surrounded
by clusters. *Too many people, too much activity,* Leo thought. He reached

for Esther's hand, needing an anchor, but it was tugged roughly away from him. He turned in time to see Ruben Miller leading her away.

"I need to talk to you, Esther," Ruben said, his tone bossy and commanding.

"No," Leo started to say, when a blurry movement to his right caught his attention. He turned in time to see Ethan streaking toward him, gun in hand, and his heart sank. The moment he had long dreaded had finally arrived; he was going to have a kill or be killed shootout with someone he had formerly considered a friend. He got the kind of focus and clarity that always consumed him before a round of action began. He was like Esther in this moment, in the zone, concentration unbreakable. There was only one thing that could interrupt his flow, or rather one person, and she was doing it now.

To his left, Esther screamed his name, panicked. He tore his attention off an advancing Ethan to her and saw her streaking toward him at a sprint, arms outstretched. And then he realized why.

Twenty paces directly in front of him, disguised as another Amish man, stood Aleksandr. His gun was aloft and pointed not at Esther, but at the center of Leo's chest.

Esther catapulted the last few steps, flung herself at him. Though she was slight, the impact of her body was enough to knock him back a step. His arms wrapped instinctively and protectively around her. A shot went off, and the world turned to chaos.

CHAPTER 26

Leo had been in plenty of civilian scenes where a gun was involved. Most of the time they had no idea. Gunshots always sounded different in real life than people thought they would. The Amish, for whom hunting was still a way of life, knew exactly what it was and began scrambling madly, scurrying back and forth, trying to figure out what happened, to help, to get out of the way. It was mass confusion, but Leo was still able to see Ethan tackle Aleksandr.

They wrestled. Leo was torn between pushing Esther away to help and holding her protectively close to usher her away. But no matter, Ethan had the situation well in hand. A few practiced jabs and kicks and their suspect was in a crumpled heap on the ground, his weapon secured, his hands bundled so tightly in zip ties his wrists began to bleed. For good measure, Ethan hobbled his ankles, trussing him like an unruly calf, before turning his attention on Leo and Esther.

"I thought it was you," Leo called. His relief at realizing Ethan had been sent there to save and not to kill them was so palpable he laughed. Ethan didn't look amused, however. He looked horror struck.

"Leo," he called, pointing. Leo looked down, and that was when he saw it, the red bloom spreading like wildfire on Esther's back.

She was so slight, so tiny, he had no idea he had been holding her upright. Now that he knew, he laid her down. Ethan was already on the phone as he ran over, giving instructions to someone.

"I had a chopper on standby," he said, but the words made no sense to Leo, nor did he care about them. All he knew was that Esther had been shot, had jumped in front of his body and taken the hit meant for him. Of course Aleksandr would want to take him out first. Without him, Esther would be easy pickings. Except she wasn't; she had the sort of strength and courage that allowed her to take a bullet for someone else, namely him. And now they were in the middle of nowhere, far away from help or a hospital. There was no way she could make it, was likely already dead.

"Lieutenant, pull yourself together," Ethan snapped, and Leo realized his hands were in his hair and he rocked back and forth, already numb with shock. The reminder that he was a marine snapped him back to focus, at least a little.

"What...what should I do?" Leo asked.

"Put pressure," Ethan said. He took Leo's hand and pressed it over the gushing hole in Esther's chest. It would have missed her heart, but what if it had hit something else? A lung, an artery? She still breathed, but barely. The way her body was arched made him believe it had hit and collapsed one of her lungs.

"Hold on, Es," he said, leaning down to whisper softly in her ear. Her eyes turned to him, a mix of panic and trust that was nearly his undoing all over again. "You're going to be all right, okay? Faith, have all your faith back, okay? Sangfroid."

She tried and failed to smile. Her lips were turning white, her face gray as her eyes fluttered.

"Hear that, Leo? That's the chopper. There's a medic on board, a former SEAL buddy of mine. She'll be at the hospital and patched up in no time, okay?"

Leo wanted to agree, to believe, to do anything but stew in the panic now dragging him under. It was happening again. He was about to lose someone on his watch, someone he cared about more than his own life, his Esther. The only coherent thought his mind seemed able to form was that if she died, he would no longer be able to survive.

His hand was slick with her blood, making it harder to keep the pressure on her wound. He was about to lose it, would forever be thankful for Ethan's calm and reassuring presence. From this point on, he would never make fun of the navy or SEALs again. *Please, please, please don't take her. Oh, God, please let her live.* Did his prayers count? He had the mad desire to beg the Amish around him to pray, but as his eyes scanned the crowd, he saw multiple heads bowed, lips murmuring. They were already praying, he was certain. *Let theirs work, even if mine don't.*

The chopper landed, the pilot and medic sprinted to their side. Ethan and the medic exchanged vital stats, hooked Esther to oxygen, and loaded her onto the chopper. It was a small chopper, no room for Leo. He remained helplessly on the ground, staring. Ethan returned to him, looking remorseful. "I can't leave until I get this wrapped up," he motioned to Aleksandr behind him. Leo had forgotten. "I'd say take my car, but I don't think you should be driving now. Hang tight, and I'll see if I can get another chopper."

Leo nodded dully. There was no way he could drive himself to the hospital, but what did it matter at this point? Of course Esther was going to die because he didn't deserve her, wasn't worthy of someone so good and selfless. "What are you doing here?" he heard himself ask. *Funny, I don't actually care why he's here.*

"Ridge kept tabs on you the whole time. The mole was Ellen."

That snapped Leo out of his haze. "Ellen? The woman who looks like someone's kindly mom?"

Ethan nodded. "She is someone's kindly mom." He motioned to Aleksandr. "He threatened to kill her granddaughter, had pictures he'd taken from inside her house. And he said if she helped him, he'd not only let her live, he'd give Ellen a half million dollars."

A half million dollars. That was what Esther's life was worth to Aleksandr, to Ellen. To Leo it was priceless. "I hope she rots in prison," Leo said.

"She probably won't," Ethan said, sighing. He swiped a hand over his face as local law enforcement pulled up. "Here's the part I hate the most." Trying to explain to overzealous country cops that you were, in fact, the good guy could sometimes be an exercise in disaster. But before Ethan could remove his ID, one of the Amish men stepped forward and spoke, filling the officer in on the story.

"Cousins," Ruben Miller crouched beside Leo and explained. "He's telling him the man shot Esther and that man tackled him. Why would someone shoot Esther?" Leo gave him a blank look. "Although he wasn't trying to shoot Esther. He tried to shoot *you*." Leo turned his face away, the knife of guilt twisting deeper. "I'll drive you to the hospital, if you want."

Leo didn't want to spend a long car ride with Ruben and his bullying suspicion, but neither did he want to stick around and wait for Ethan to tie things up. Wordlessly, he tossed Ethan a nod, stood, and followed Ruben to his truck. *Maybe he's expended all his words and the ride will be silent.*

"I called Esther's dad."

No such luck on the silence. Leo blew out a breath. "Why?"

"Because something doesn't add up. She shows up here in the middle of our engagement so-called married to a guy like you?"

"What do you mean a guy like me?" he asked, bridge of his nose pinched tightly.

"Someone normal."

"What do you mean normal? Why would I not be normal?"

"Maybe you don't know, but Esther has the autism." He stated it as if imparting a state secret.

"Of course I know, and I don't care. And why do you care if you wanted to marry her so badly?" Leo asked.

"I had an obligation. Our families go back a long ways," Ruben said.

Leo began to see how Esther's life might have played out, with Ruben playing the martyr for their entire marriage because he'd done the great deed of taking her on, burden as she was. He would have bullied and battered her until she broke which, knowing her, wouldn't take long. Something she said to him when they first met made more sense. *There are different kinds of pain, Leo.* Not only had she not loved this man, she had known how he viewed her, as less than. "I *didn't* have an obligation. I adore her, she's my heart, my whole world." His voice broke and he stared out the window, swallowing convulsively.

"Her father doesn't believe you're married, said it must have been some kind of work assignment."

Leo blew out a breath but otherwise didn't reply. What could he say? He couldn't continue to lie when it was about to be outed as a falsehood.

"I suppose our engagement is still on," Ruben said.

"Read the room, moron," Leo muttered.

"What?" Ruben said.

Leo faced him. "Let me be extremely clear for your tiny bowl haircut brain. Esther is off limits to you, now and forevermore. Don't talk to her, don't come near her, and if you even so much as think about touching her, I will ensure it's the last thing you ever do. I know twenty ways to kill a man, and I swear I'll use the slowest and most painful one on you."

"You can't tell me what to do," Ruben said, suspender-clad chest puffing.

"Try me," Leo said. Maybe whatever Ruben read in his face convinced him or he merely thought Leo was deranged. Either way, he shut up and faced forward the remainder of the drive.

CHAPTER 27

The hospital was more than an hour away in Buffalo. The flight had probably taken no time, as Ethan said. Leo stalked to the emergency room in a frenzy and felt zero shame about identifying himself as her husband. It was a lucky break that, after so many weeks of working together, he knew most of the pertinent details of her life, such as address, phone number, birthdate, and insurance carrier. She had no allergies and no medical history to speak of. It felt good to be able to fill out the forms, to stake a tangible piece of Esther as proof of their close relationship. *Take that, Ruben, you suspender-wearing freak.* The freak in question was nowhere to be found. Leo supposed he should feel bad about threatening the guy who gave him a ride and then storming off without a word of thanks, but he didn't. Somehow Ruben now felt tied up with Aleksandr in his mind. They were both a threat to Esther, one to her physical safety and the other to her emotional wellbeing.

For two hours, Leo heard nothing, despite asking so many times he probably wore a path from his chair to the desk. All he knew was that she was in surgery. "We'll let you know," was now his least favorite phrase.

Ethan arrived at the end of those two hours, looking grim and exhausted. He sank into the chair beside Leo with a sigh. "News?"

"Nope."

He sighed again. "Man, I hate hospitals."

"Yep."

"And waiting."

"Yep."

"Ridge isn't coming, by the way. Doesn't even know any of this is going on. Maggie was in labor when I left. I figure I'll give them a chance to emerge from the fog of new-baby bliss before I spring this on him. Maybe by then I'll be able to convey the good news of her prognosis."

"Who's in charge when he's away?" Leo asked, stretching his legs out in front of him. Once again he was ridiculously thankful for Ethan's presence. He was the kind of person who was good at providing a distraction, when one was needed.

"I am," Ethan said, shuddering. "No idea how that happened. I hate being the go-to guy for stuff. So much more fun to be in the field."

"Which field are you in?" Leo asked, feeling about a thousand years old.

"I felt a bit like you a couple of years ago and then…" he cut off and shook his head. "Nah, it's going to sound dumb."

"Dumb is so much better than anything else I've got right now," Leo informed him.

Ethan shrugged. "I met Amelia, fell in love, got married. Suddenly the work didn't seem so soul crushing anymore."

"Women," Leo said, but not in a disgusted way. More awed.

"Women," Ethan agreed in the same tone. "Esther's a cutie, by the way. She reminds me of this girl I knew in high school. One of the smartest chicks I've ever met and so ridiculously clueless about life. I used to pull pranks on her all the time because she was the sort of person who didn't take it personally, who could laugh at herself. She was good people."

"Esther's good people," Leo said.

"With so few of those in the world, we have to hold on to the ones we find," Ethan said.

Leo didn't reply. Everything felt thick and heavy, his eyes, his throat, his nose.

"I really think she's going to be fine, and I'm not blowing smoke. I've seen a lot of wounds. That looked like the kind that appears more dramatic than it actually is, for real. And I know my buddy pretty well. He was serious but not freaked. If he'd thought she wasn't going to make it, he would have been freaked. Has a real soft spot for the ladies." Ethan said. He stretched. A woman who walked nearby did a double take and walked into a wall. Ethan didn't even notice. Though they hadn't been close, he and Ethan had been acquaintances for a long time, had worked some ops at the same time. Ethan had always been a player. To not even see him react to the woman now was nothing short of miraculous.

"How'd you know Amelia was the one?" Leo asked.

Ethan didn't bat a lash at the personal question. Soldiers in foxholes can talk about anything with no judgment. "Because she was the one I couldn't live without."

Leo thought about his desperate prayer, his certainty he couldn't survive if anything happened to Esther.

"Mr. Stoltzfus." A man in scrubs entered the waiting room and Leo stood. "Hi, I'm Dr. Midrihani. Your wife is out of surgery and in recovery. She'll spend the night in ICU where she'll have limited visitation, no one besides you allowed. If all goes well, we'll move her to another floor tomorrow."

"She's going to be okay?"

"The bullet punctured her lung and caused a tension pneumothorax. That caused pressure on her breathing and heart and was likely the cause of her extreme discomfort and any other symptoms you saw. We inserted a chest tube to re-inflate her lung and relieve the pressure. We'll monitor her, but with no complications I expect her to go home in a few days and be back to normal in a couple of weeks."

Leo couldn't believe it. He shook the man's hand, but he had no idea if he thanked him. He hoped so because he was thankful. Beyond, really. He fell into the chair beside Ethan again, staring dazedly into space while Ethan made the call to Ridge. *She's really okay,* he thought, so thankful that now he was the one who had trouble catching his breath.

Ethan finished his call on a yawn.

"You should go, I've got this," Leo said.

"I can stay as long as you need," Ethan said and, to his credit, sounded sincere.

"I've got it from here, really. You should be there to meet Maggie's baby."

Ethan grinned. "He's a bruiser. I'm not sure Ridge actually comprehended anything I just said to him."

"Of course he did," Leo said. "Ridge is always the job."

"Nah, that was PM, pre-Maggie. If you just heard what I just heard, you'd have your doubts, too."

They were quiet a few beats before Leo spoke again. "You think The Colonel is ever not the job?"

"Nah," they said together after a few seconds deliberation. It was too hard to imagine their tough-as-nails boss as anything less than the absolute rock he'd always been.

"Probably came out of his mom in full uniform," Ethan said.

"Saluting," Leo added, and they snickered. It felt good to laugh. A minute later, they called his name again. He stood. "Have a good trip back and, Ethan, thanks. For everything. I owe you."

"No, you don't," Ethan said. "You're on my team; that makes us brothers."

It was a corny thing to say, or would have been, if Leo didn't know how much he meant it. He hadn't had that sort of brotherhood since half his team was killed in a mission gone wrong, and he hadn't realized how much he'd missed it, nor how good it would feel to have it back again. They fist bumped, which for them was as good as a sobbing hug, and Leo went in search of Esther.

*S*he looked even smaller than normal, diminished somehow by her ordeal. Her face was as white as the sheet behind her. A tube stuck out of her mouth, its rhythmic beeping more ominous than comforting. They warned him she would likely be out all night from the trauma, blood loss, and anesthesia. Leo crept close and sat silently in the chair beside her bed.

He didn't know what to say, so he didn't say anything. Instead he pressed his face to her leg and cried, hard. He wept like a small child, until he was empty and drained of everything. Spent, exhausted, wiped clean of every emotion, he finally fell asleep.

When he woke, The Colonel was there, standing across from him on the other side of Esther's bed, staring ponderously down at Leo. Somehow Leo refrained from flinching, a thing everyone who knew him longer than a minute realized was an annoyance. "Sir," he croaked.

The Colonel nodded at him. "How are you holding up?"

Leo glanced at Esther, still unconscious between them. "Esther's the one...the one who..." his voice broke and he took a shaky breath. "Not well."

"It seems she's going to be okay."

"Yes, sir."

"I'm sending her to Quantico, when she's recovered."

Leo's eyes snapped back to him. "Sir?"

"Ridge assures me she's a much-needed asset to the team, almost invaluable, it seems. If we're going to keep her, she's going to need to learn a few things, more than one man can teach her."

"She's a pacifist, sir," Leo replied. Esther at Quantico? There was so much knowledge to be absorbed; she would love it. His mouth quirked at the prospect of her coming excitement.

"Pacifists can shoot targets. I'll have a word with them about the hand-to-hand."

"I'd appreciate that, sir," Leo said. Somehow, despite not embracing authority, Leo never had to remind himself to call The Colonel "sir." It came as natural as breathing.

"And what are you going to do?" The Colonel asked, as if Leo had a choice when, really, the man was his boss. It was basically up to him where he went next. Unless…was he actually giving him the option to leave, to walk away?

"I…I don't honestly know, sir. I…" he chanced a glance at The Colonel and saw an unwavering gaze in return—no anger or judgment, merely mild curiosity. "I'm tired."

The Colonel nodded once and pinned Leo with a stare. "I'm about to impart to you the only bit of personal information I will share for the rest of our lives, so listen well. Everyone believes I'm insane, and I don't care. Because the truth is I'm the sanest man you ever met, and there's one simple reason: my wife and daughters. Without them, I would have lost my mind decades ago. It's a hard game we play, Lieutenant, made nearly impossible without good people by your side. Surround yourself well, and you'll be okay."

"Yes, sir," Leo said, both confused and inspired.

"It would seem you're going to have about five months of free time to make some decisions," The Colonel said. Quantico was twenty weeks, and visitors wouldn't be allowed. The thought of being away from Esther for so long was impossibly painful, and yet maybe it was for the best.

Leo's glance slid from Esther to The Colonel, but the man was gone. *How does he do that,* Leo wondered. With nothing left to do but wait, he laid his head down again and closed his eyes.

CHAPTER 28

Six Months Later

Home. The word had taken on a different meaning in the months following Leo's time in the cabin. He was back in the states after his latest assignment in Cairo, back in his crummy apartment, back in his uncomfortable, lonely bed. But he wasn't home.

He had done his best to make his living situation better. The night he left Esther in Buffalo, the night her father and mother showed up at the hospital, relieving him of watch, he flew back to DC with every intention of getting so drunk he would forget everything. Everything that happened the day Esther was shot, everything that happened after, basically everything that happened in his entire life.

But as he walked through the airport, intent on grabbing a cab and heading to the liquor store within walking distance of his house, he stopped short and backed up, his attention caught by a title at an airport newsstand. *Home Building 101.* Huh. Wouldn't hurt to give it a scan. He picked it up and grabbed a cab, not noticing until he lay in bed that he had told the cabbie to take him home, minus the booze.

The next morning he woke and cleaned his hovel of an apartment. He did four loads of laundry and took out the trash. He could only locate two fitted sheets, but at least they were clean. That night he went out and bought another book, *Home Design for Beginners.*

He began physical therapy the following day. Two weeks after that he was cleared of desk duty and resumed his former job.

In the interim, all these many weeks later, his apartment remained immaculate, his laundry caught up. He hadn't taken a drink, had kept his nose clean and showed up for every commitment on time. And he had never been more miserably alone and jaded.

He tossed his jacket on the chair, opened the fridge, and stared at its miserable contents. Despite doing a better job of being a grownup, his food-seeking skills had not improved. His refrigerator remained stereotypical bachelor fare, but Leo reasoned it was the fault of his job, which took him out of the state and often out of the country for long stretches at a time. He reached for a jar of jam, intending to make peanut better and jelly, when the voice spoke.

"PB&J, what are you, twelve?"

He slammed the door closed and swiveled to face the room. Cameron Ridge sat on his couch, ankle propped casually over his knee.

"You're actually trying to turn into the old man," Leo accused, resisting the urge to press his hand to his heart.

"If I'm lucky," Ridge said casually. He uncrossed his leg and sat forward, propping his forearms on his thighs. "How you doing, Leo?"

"Minus the heart failure, I'm good."

Ridge grinned. "I'll take the heart failure as a compliment."

"You would," Leo said. He grabbed the jar of peanut butter and a spoon, deciding to bypass the jam and bread. He plopped onto the couch across from Ridge and swallowed his mouthful of peanut butter. "What's up, pretty boy?"

"Is that any way to speak to your superior?"

Leo froze. "I don't work for you any more."

"No, you don't," Ridge said. "You know why I used to hate you, Leo?"

"Jealousy?" Leo guessed, somewhat hopefully.

Ridge laughed. "No. It was because you were lazy, sloppy, entitled, selfish, reckless, and a hot head. And those were your finer qualities."

"Is that why you took Cassie?" Leo asked, bringing up the oldest and biggest resentment.

"Yep. I didn't love her, but I liked her, and it was better to date her for a month than see her wasted on you."

"And everyone thinks you're so nice," Leo said, sticking the spoon back in the jar for another scoop.

"I am nice. I'm also a pretty good boss, which is why I'm here, because one of my employees is not performing up to par. I'm pretty sure you know which one."

Leo shifted uncomfortably. "Esther?" Would it always hurt to say her name?

Ridge nodded.

"What's wrong with her? Don't tell me she's not performing well because I won't believe it. She's too focused."

"You're right. She's too focused. Know what I found yesterday morning when I arrived at work?"

Leo blinked at him, unwilling to say it.

"You know, I kind of pride myself on being the first one there and the last one to leave. Like the captain of the Titanic. So imagine my surprise when I walked in and found Esther at her desk."

"She beat you?"

"No, she never left from the night before, worked all night. I don't even think she realized night had passed."

"Oh," Leo said, a sinking feeling vying with a bloom of hope in the pit of his stomach.

"It's the third time it happened since she returned from Quantico."

"But that's only been three weeks," Leo said.

Ridge gave him a knowing smile. "Look who has her schedule memorized."

Leo cleared his throat. "I keep tabs. She was the job, I like to make sure she's okay."

"She's not okay."

"I'm not sure that's my responsibility anymore," Leo said.

"Amelia cut her hair," Ridge tossed out and Leo gasped as if he'd been stabbed. "And the rumor around the office is that a guard asked her out."

"Did...did she go?"

Ridge shrugged.

Leo's heart thudded, but he couldn't, wouldn't inflict himself on Esther again. "You should get someone else, someone better suited."

"There's no one better suited, no one who knows her as well, knows how to handle her. We've all made our strides and she's settling in nicely, but it's not the same and you know it."

"You said yourself all the reasons I'm a screwup," Leo said, miserable to have to admit the truth in front of his former rival.

"No, I said you were a screwup, *were*. The man you were under my roof was not the same kid I knew back in the day. And, not to get all blubbery on you, Lieutenant, but I kind of like the new Leo. Good guy, this one, conscientious, protective, a team player, way more humble, willing to admit when he's wrong or ask for help. He's the kind of guy I need on a permanent basis."

"Are you offering me a job or hitting on me?" Leo demanded.

"I've lost so much sleep since the baby arrived, it's hard to tell," Ridge said, smothering a yawn. "The point is I'm offering you an opportunity here to do what you do best."

"Babysit?" Leo said, aiming for snide and falling short.

"Handle with care. And occasionally I might stick you in the field with Ethan. Boy's getting tired of being our lone runner, and you two seem to have a flow together."

Leo twirled the spoon in the container without really seeing it. "I'll think about it." He glanced back up at Ridge, but too late. The room was now empty.

CHAPTER 29

W hen Leo walked into the office, seemingly everyone turned to stare, everyone except the person he most wanted to see. Esther, he knew, would be in the zone. It would take something special and unexpected to snap her out of it. He shuffled the tidy stack of papers in his fingers and marched determinedly forward.

She sat with her back to him in their former cubicle, hair significantly shorter but still long. He sighed a note of relief. Same hair, same Esther. He took a piece of paper from the stack and set it before her, waiting for her to read it.

Absquatulate: to leave without saying goodbye.

Her shoulders stiffened and she turned, facing him. He held up the next paper in his stack.

Tacenda: Things better left unsaid.

And the next, and then the others, holding them aloft like flashcards.

Cimmerian: very dark, gloomy.

Toska: A dull ache of the soul, a sick pining, spiritual anguish.

Lacuna: A blank space, a missing part.

Seelenverwandt: Two souls who are not blood related but are two of a kind.

Sarang: The feeling of wanting to be with someone until death.

Redamancy: The act of loving the one who loves you; a love returned in full.

He set the stack of papers aside and waited for some reaction. He had walked out on her when she was still unconscious, abandoned her to her father's care without a word because he was too afraid to stay and face her, too guilty she'd taken a bullet meant for him, too certain of his own deficiencies. He was out of the room getting a coffee when her parents arrived. By the time he returned they had settled in and reclaimed ownership of her. Leo had hovered in the doorway, watching unobserved while her mother pressed a tender hand to her forehead and her father clasped her hand protectively. *Why does she need me when she has them and they do such a better job of taking care of her,* he wondered. Then he eased away and disappeared. And now he was back, and did she hate him? She should.

Wordlessly, she reached behind her and withdrew a book. *Homebuilding For Dummies,* only she had used a marker to scratch out "Dummies" and written "Leo" instead.

She knew. Somehow, she knew even before he did that he wouldn't fall apart and revert to old ways, that he would continue with the plan, begin to save money, get his life in order, and plan for his future home. She had more faith in him than he did, as ever.

"I'm sorry," he whispered.

"I know," she said.

"I just needed to..."

She pressed her fingers to his lips. "Leo, I *know*. It's okay. I recovered, I went to Quantico. I haven't exactly been idle in your absence. I'm not one of those women who falls apart without my man."

"You cut your hair," he said, touching the ends. It was so much curlier and more buoyant now.

"Oh, right. Amelia's very persuasive. She cornered me at a party."

"I love it, she was right. It suits you. You went to a party?"

"Yes, and I didn't blurt anything alienating. At least I don't think I did. I do remember quoting the stats on salmonella when the egg salad sat out past the three hour mark, but no one seemed to mind that helpful tidbit," she said.

He laughed and suddenly Babs and Blue popped over the adjoining cubicle like prairie dogs. "Hey, Leo," Blue said. The two wore matching, ornery grins. Clearly they'd been eavesdropping the entire time. "Did Esther tell you I'm getting married next weekend? She's going to need a date."

"The security guard's not available?" Leo asked, tone turning crisp with jealousy.

"Aw, snap," Babs muttered.

"You mean Hank? He's sixty, if he's a day, although he did propose after I brought him some of my homemade cinnamon bread," Esther said.

Leo scowled. "Stupid Ridge." He had purposely taunted him to make him jealous. And, like an idiot, it worked. There was so much more to say, but Babs and Blue were both still grinning goofily.

"The happily ever after is my favorite part," Blue said.

"For sure," Babs agreed, and they high fived.

"Maybe we could move this into the soundproof room with the door," Leo said, taking Esther's hand and leading her away.

"Don't be like that. We'll go back to pretending we're not hanging on every word," Babs called.

"You better not run off and get married before next weekend. Jane will literally kill me," Blue added.

Esther, chuckling, trotted to keep up with his long strides. Leo opened the door, herded her inside, and leaned on it when it was closed. And then at long last he did what he had been longing and aching and itching to do the longest six months of his life—he gathered her up in an enveloping hug and stuffed his face to her neck, inhaling. *Home.* Esther was the missing ingredient in every plan, every design, every plot of land he'd inspected and rejected. The *Dawdy haus* wasn't a magical healing field because it was isolated, it was always because Esther was there. Home was not a place, it was a person, this person, *his* person.

"I feel like I can finally breathe again," he said, words muffled by her throat.

"I missed you," she said, flat and expressionless, and he smiled. If he didn't know her, he might think it was a rebuff, but he did know her and therefore read all she left unsaid.

He pulled back and kissed her wet cheeks. "I'm sorry."

"Me, too," she said.

"Why are you sorry?"

"Because you've been going through things without me there to care for you," she said.

He took a breath, the first deep one in half a year, and let it out slowly. And then he had to sit down because it was too much all at once and he felt like he might buckle from the weight of joy and relief. Esther sat in his lap but, unlike her previously chaste side-saddle arrangement, straddled him, putting them intimately face to face.

"How are you? How's the lung?" he asked, touching a finger in the center of her chest, his finger smoothing lightly over a puckered scar.

"It's good, I'm fine."

He tipped his head at her.

"No, really, I am. Running at Quantico was a bit of a strain, I got a little breathless. But someone must have warned them because no one gave me a hard time about it. And they didn't make me fight."

"Did you love it? I want to hear everything," he said.

"I loved it. I'll tell you all I can remember."

"You remember everything."

"It's going to be a long conversation. What about you? What's been happening?"

"Let's see, you took a bullet meant for me, but it didn't matter because I'm the one who died. I've been in a coma the last six months, and now I'm awake again. The end."

"That is not true. I am not the center of your universe."

"Aren't you? You could have fooled me," he said. "That day at the thrift store, when you told those girls the story of how we met, you weren't lying, were you? You knew from the beginning about us."

"Yes. I'm not what you'd call intuitive, thanks to this whole autism thing." She waved her hand in front of her face. "But I saw you in that airport, and I knew we belonged to each other."

"Then why did you try to set me up with the baby store girl?" he asked, exasperated.

"Because I didn't have a crush on you, at least not then. I thought we would be the sort of friends who always took care of each other. It never occurred to me we would fall in love. I thought I was unlovable."

"I thought *I* was unlovable."

"I'm glad we proved each other wrong," she said. He bent to kiss her, but she pulled away. "Wait, I have to tell you something."

"What?"

"I held Ridge and Maggie's baby."

"Okay."

"I've held 168 babies in my lifetime, an actual number because I count all the things. My mom was always handing me a sibling or cousin or baby she delivered in the hope that it would spark some sense of normalcy in my broken brain, that suddenly I would want to be a wife and mom, give up career notions, and settle down with full feelings like an actual girl."

"Didn't happen?" he guessed.

"Not once, but apparently the 169th baby is the charm. He has Ridge's looks and Maggie's sweetness."

Leo scowled. "You think Ridge is nice looking?"

"Leo, Ridge is indisputably one of the prettiest humans I've ever seen. The proportionality of his face could launch a doctoral thesis in mathematics. But you are the only man I have ever loved, will ever love, could ever love, so your jealousy is sort of wasted effort."

"Point taken," he said. "You were holding Ridge and Maggie's bundle of joy and feeling…"

"That's it, I was feeling. Usually to me, holding a baby is like holding a bag of wet flour. I literally couldn't care less about what's in my hands. But this time my heart started to flutter. It was like being shot all over again because for the first time I pictured our baby, yours and mine, and I think I might want that. I know you're not big into kids or parenthood, but I needed to let you know it's on the table now."

The thought of being someone's father sent him into a panic spiral. He wasn't ready, might never be ready, would royally screw it up. But then he pictured Esther, her belly round with his baby, their baby, and his heart also stuttered. "It's something to discuss," he said, pressing his palm on her belly, heart thudding. "But you know, Esther, there's really only one way to get a baby."

"Get married?"

"Yes, but after that."

"This seems like a good time to tell you I got a new book."

He smiled, her tone telling him he was going to like what he was about to hear. "Yeah?"

"It's similar to the one my mom got me but, um, better, I think."

"Not gross?" he asked.

She shook her head. "A little scary, but wholly intriguing."

"Everything that is within me seems programmed to take care of you in every way. I promise it will not be scary, okay?"

She nodded. "I liked your words," she whispered shyly.

"It was how I coped with being apart. I collected words to try and patch the missing pieces inside me. Didn't work, but I found some to give to you."

"I collected some words, too," she said.

"For me?" he asked.

"No, for the people who wrote the kissing book. I thought I would write and tell them there are so many better options than fruits and vegetables."

He was beaming like the love-addled idiot he was. To think he would get to partake of her for the rest of his life was an unspeakable and overwhelming gift he in no way deserved. "What words?"

She leaned closer and let her lips brush his as she spoke. "Mellifluous, perspicacious, onomatopoeia, recalibration, indivisible, paleopidemiological. Shall I go on?"

"Have mercy, Esther," he croaked, sweating.

"Okay, Leo," she replied and kissed him.

*T*hank you for reading *The Finder and The Keeper,* the eighth book in the Spies Like Us series. For more books, please visit my website at www.vanessagraybartal.com

ABOUT THE AUTHOR

Vanessa Gray Bartal is a foodie who spends her time trolling bakeries and dreaming of new ways to use sourdough. When she is not baking (or eating), she loves to make music and spend time with her husband, three children, and sheepadoodle in rural Ohio. Her dream is to fill her books with enough coziness and warmth to brighten someone's day and make them smile. She would love to hear from you on Facebook or through email.

Printed in Great Britain
by Amazon

59567754R10108